# Palette of Intrigue - A Female-Led Mystery Unveiling Barcelona Art Scene

Adela Vesper

Published by Palette of Intrigue, 2024.

PALETTE OF INTRIGUE - A FEMALE-LED MYSTERY UNVEILING BARCELONA ART SCENE

**First edition. May 6, 2024.**

Copyright © 2024 Adela Vesper.

ISBN: 979-8224480388

Written by Adela Vesper.

# Chapter 1: The Uninvited

IN THE VIBRANT HEART of Barcelona, where the pulse of modernity beats in harmony with the echoes of ancient streets, Mia Valdés prepared her canvas with the meticulous care of a seasoned artist. Her studio, nestled in a quaint corner of the Gothic Quarter, was a sanctuary of scattered paint tubes, brushes of every size, and canvases that bore the soulful burden of her abstract dreams.

The morning sun filtered through the tall, narrow windows, casting long shadows that danced upon the exposed brick walls. Mia, with her dark hair pulled back into a careless bun, stood back to assess the large canvas before her. This piece would be the centerpiece of her upcoming debut exhibition—a collection that had already begun to stir whispers among Barcelona's eclectic art circles.

As she dabbed her brush into the vibrant cobalt blue, her phone buzzed insistently. Mia glanced at it, her focus momentarily broken. The caller ID flashed an unknown number. With a reluctant sigh, she wiped her hands on her apron and answered.

"Hello?"

"Mia Valdés?" The voice on the other end was clipped, unfamiliar.

"Yes, speaking. Who is this?"

"My name is Inspector Llorente. I'm afraid I have some unsettling news concerning a close associate of yours, Esteban Ruiz."

Mia's heart skipped a beat. Esteban, her mentor and the esteemed curator of her exhibition, was more than a mere associate. He was her guiding light in the labyrinthine world of art.

"What happened to him?" Her voice was a mix of worry and dread.

"I'm sorry to inform you that Mr. Ruiz was found dead early this morning at his residence. We are treating the circumstances surrounding his death as suspicious."

The room seemed to spin around Mia as she clutched the phone tighter. "Dead? But I just spoke to him last night about the exhibition..."

"We would like to ask you some questions, Miss Valdés. It would be best if we could meet in person. Are you available today?"

"Yes, of course," Mia managed to reply, her mind racing.

"Thank you. I will be at your studio within the hour."

As she hung up, the brushes, the paints, the unfinished masterpiece—all seemed trivial in the shadow of such tragic news. Mia felt a chill run through her despite the warmth of the morning sun. She knew that Barcelona, for all its beauty, had undercurrents that could pull anyone into its depths. Esteban had often hinted at tensions within the art world, a place rife with jealousy and often, unspoken secrets.

Now, with his sudden demise, Mia had to navigate these troubled waters alone, her only aid being her acute perception and the colors that spoke a language only she could understand. As she waited for Inspector Llorente, her mind wandered to the last conversation she had with Esteban. Had he mentioned anything unusual? Any hint of worry about something—or someone—that might have posed a threat?

With a deep breath, Mia prepared herself for the inspector's arrival. This exhibition, meant to be her grand unveiling, might now reveal more than her artistic debut. It could uncover a web of deceit and danger that had operated unseen amidst the gilded frames of Barcelona's art scene.

As she pondered, Mia realized that the mystery she needed to solve was not just on her canvases, but entangled in the very fabric of her life. The journey ahead promised to be as tumultuous and unpredictable as the abstract swirls of paint that defined her art. And somewhere within that chaos, she hoped to find not only the truth behind Esteban's death but also the essence of her own strength.

As the footsteps echoed in the corridor approaching her studio, Mia steeled herself. The door was about to open on a chapter of her life that would challenge every stroke of her brush and every shade of her soul.

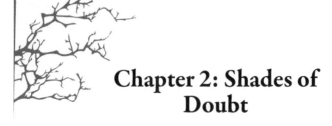

# Chapter 2: Shades of Doubt

Mia's heart pounded in rhythm with the approaching footsteps. The old wooden door creaked open, and a tall figure silhouetted against the bright Spanish sun stepped into the cool dimness of her studio. Inspector Carlos Llorente, his features sharp and his gaze penetrating, scanned the room with an air of calculated observation before settling on Mia.

"Miss Valdés, thank you for agreeing to speak with me on such short notice." His voice was deep, laced with a formal politeness that did little to ease the tension.

Mia nodded, her eyes tracing the contours of his solemn face, searching for a hint of compassion. "How did it happen?" she asked, her voice steady despite the turmoil inside her.

"We believe it was an accident. He was found at the bottom of his staircase. Initial indications suggest he might have fallen," Llorente explained, watching her closely, as if looking for a crack in her composed façade.

"A fall..." Mia echoed, her mind racing. Esteban, with his usual meticulous attention to detail, was not one to trip and fall, especially not in his own home, a place he navigated as easily as his own gallery.

"Yes, but we are keeping all possibilities open. Now, if you don't mind, I would like to ask about your relationship with Mr. Ruiz." His eyes locked onto hers, a flicker of curiosity beneath his professional detachment.

Mia felt a strange and unexpected tension rise between them, his proximity unsettling her more than the questions he posed. "He was my mentor and friend. He was helping me prepare for the exhibition."

"Was anyone else present during your last conversation with him?"

"No, we were alone here." Mia gestured to the surrounding chaos of her studio. "He was excited about the show. He said it would be a sensation."

Inspector Llorente scribbled something in his notebook, then paused, his gaze lingering a moment too long in what seemed like a blend of professional scrutiny and personal interest. "Was there anyone who might have wished harm upon him? Perhaps an artist he rejected or a deal that went sour?"

Mia shrugged, the weight of suspicion heavy in the air. "The art world can be cutthroat, but I can't imagine it leading to this."

"Understood. We'll need a list of people who were close to him, anyone who might know more." His tone was insistent, yet there was a softness in his eyes that suggested a depth of empathy.

Just then, the door burst open, and in strode Javier, his dark curls tousled as if he'd rushed here, his face etched with concern. "Mia, I came as soon as I heard. Are you okay?" He glanced between Mia and the inspector, his arrival slicing through the tension.

Mia forced a smile, feeling torn between Javier's familiar warmth and the intriguing yet disconcerting presence of Inspector Llorente. "Yes, I'm okay, Javi. Inspector Llorente was just asking some questions about Esteban."

Javier nodded, offering a handshake to the inspector, who accepted it with a polite nod. "I hope you find whoever is responsible," Javier said, his voice firm.

"I intend to," Llorente replied, his gaze flitting between Mia and Javier, an unreadable expression crossing his face.

As the inspector made his leave, promising to return if further questions arose, Mia felt Javier's arm slip around her shoulders, a protective gesture that she would normally find comforting. Yet, her thoughts lingered on the inspector's lingering looks, stirring a confusion of emotions that she couldn't quite decipher.

Alone again, Javier's presence felt overwhelmingly close. "Mia, whatever you need, I'm here," he murmured, pressing a kiss to her temple.

"Thank you, Javi. I just... I need to understand what happened to Esteban," she whispered, her mind a whirl of dark canvases and darker possibilities.

As Javier held her, Mia's eyes settled on her unfinished painting, the chaotic swirls of color mirroring the turmoil within her. With Esteban's death cloaked in mystery and an unsettling attraction to the inspector clouding her thoughts, Mia knew she was on the brink of a profound unraveling, both of her life and the secrets that lay hidden within the shadows of Barcelona's art scene.

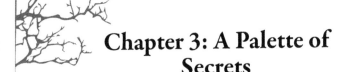

# Chapter 3: A Palette of Secrets

The late afternoon sun cast long shadows across Mia's studio, illuminating the vivid chaos of her art. Canvases stood like silent sentinels around the room, each one a testament to her tumultuous emotions—a whirlwind of azure and scarlet, interspersed with violent streaks of black and soothing patches of white. The colors bled into each other, much like the merging uncertainties of Mia's life.

Javier leaned against the worn wooden easel, his gaze lingering not on Mia but on the chaotic imagery splattered across the canvas before him. "These are getting intense, Mia," he remarked, his tone a mix of admiration and concern. "They're almost... visceral."

Mia, her hands stained with paint, continued to add touches to a particularly stormy section of her latest piece, her movements deliberate and a bit more forceful than necessary. "It's just a reflection of what I'm feeling these days," she replied without meeting his eyes.

Javier's presence had always been a calming one, akin to the steadying touch of a lighthouse beam across stormy seas. Today, however, there was something different about him—something unsettling that Mia couldn't quite place. Perhaps it was the subtle shift in his demeanor, or the faint hint of something concealed behind his usual warmth.

"Mia," Javier began, hesitating as he chose his words carefully. "About Esteban... You know you can tell me anything, right?"

Mia stopped painting, her brush suspended in mid-air. "Of course, Javi. Why do you ask?"

"It's just that... Well, you and he were close. And sometimes, people get the wrong idea about relationships like that." Javier's gaze was fixed, searching.

Mia felt a prickle of defensiveness. "What are you implying?" Her voice was sharper than she intended.

"No, no, I didn't mean to imply anything untoward!" Javier quickly amended, his hands raised in a placating gesture. "I'm just worried about how this might affect you, especially with the police sniffing around."

The tension eased slightly as Mia resumed her painting, though her strokes were now less sure, her thoughts clouded with doubt about Javier's sudden concern. "The police think it was an accident," she said, though her voice carried a trace of uncertainty.

Javier nodded slowly, his eyes not leaving her face. "If there's anything you haven't told me about that night..."

Mia's brush clattered to the floor, splattering droplets of cobalt blue across the aged tiles. "Javier, are you asking if I had something to do with Esteban's death?"

"No!" His response was immediate, his expression one of shock. "I just mean if there's anything that could help understand what happened..."

Collecting herself, Mia bent to pick up her brush, her hands trembling slightly. "I told the inspector everything. There's nothing more."

Javier moved closer, his demeanor softening. "I'm sorry, Mia. I didn't mean to upset you. It's just all this talk of accidents and investigations—it has me on edge."

Mia nodded, her expression weary. "I know, me too. Let's not fall into a pit of suspicion ourselves, okay? We need to trust each other, especially now."

Javier reached out to gently squeeze her shoulder, an attempt to bridge the gap that had formed between them. "Of course. I trust you, Mia. More than anyone."

As he left the studio, Mia's gaze drifted back to her unfinished painting. The colors seemed more somber now, the forms more menacing. She realized that the suspicion and secrets seeping into her life were coloring her art, each stroke a revelation of her deepest fears.

In the solitude of her studio, surrounded by the vivid declarations of her inner turmoil, Mia felt the weight of uncertainty heavier than ever. If Javier harbored doubts, what would others think? And deep down, amidst the swirl of colors on her canvas, did she harbor her own doubts about the night Esteban died?

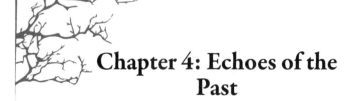

# Chapter 4: Echoes of the Past

The evening draped Barcelona in a velvet cloak of indigo and gold, the lights of the city flickering like distant stars brought down to earth. In her studio, surrounded by the sentinel-like presence of her canvases, Mia found no comfort in the night's artistic whisper. Her thoughts, instead, were ensnared by the events of the past few days—the death of Esteban, the unsettling inquiries of Inspector Llorente, and Javier's strange, probing questions.

Restlessness drove her from her stool by the window. Mia moved around the studio, adjusting a canvas here, straightening a paint tube there, her actions mechanical and devoid of the usual passion her art evoked. The sharp ring of the telephone shattered the monotonous silence, causing her to flinch slightly before she answered it.

"Mia, it's Clara," came the anxious voice of her friend, a fellow artist who had studied under Esteban's critical yet nurturing eye. "Have you heard? The police—they've been asking about him, about all of us who were close to him."

Mia leaned against the wall, her hand tightening around the receiver. "Yes, they've already been here. They think it was an accident, but they're investigating everything and everyone connected to him."

Clara's breath hitched audibly over the line. "But that's just it, Mia. I've heard things... whispers that maybe it wasn't an accident. That someone might have had a reason to want Esteban gone."

The statement hung between them like a dark cloud. Mia felt a cold dread settle in her stomach. "Clara, we shouldn't jump to conclusions without evidence."

"I know, I know," Clara sighed. "It's just—Esteban was involved in some pretty heated dealings recently. Some art deals that didn't go well. People are talking."

Mia considered this new information, her mind racing. Esteban had always been discreet about the business side of the art world, shielding his protégés from the harsher realities of their chosen profession. "Did he ever mention anything to you about problems? Anyone who might have had a grudge?"

There was a pause, then Clara replied hesitantly, "He did mention a few names now and then, said they were untrustworthy. But you know how he was—always a bit secretive about the details."

"Yes, I know." Mia's gaze drifted to a painting, half-concealed in shadow, its tumultuous whirls of color reflecting her current turmoil. "Clara, could you do me a favor? Could you find out more about these dealings, about the people he mentioned?"

"Of course, Mia. I'll see what I can dig up. We need to stick together in this."

After hanging up, Mia sat back down, her mind abuzz with possibilities. If Esteban had enemies capable of murder, the implications were chilling. And where did that leave her? As his protégé, might she too be in danger?

A soft knock at the door jolted her from her thoughts. She rose to answer it, finding Inspector Llorente on the threshold, his presence as imposing as ever. "Miss Valdés," he greeted, his hat in hand, "I hope I'm not intruding. I thought it pertinent to inform you personally—there have been developments in Mr. Ruiz's case."

Mia felt her heartbeat quicken. "Developments?"

"We've obtained evidence that might suggest foul play. It appears Mr. Ruiz may have been pushed down the stairs."

The room seemed to spin slightly as she processed his words. Pushed? The implication that someone had indeed intended to harm Esteban was horrifying yet strangely vindicating—her instincts had been correct.

"I see," Mia managed to say, steadying herself against the doorframe. "Do you have any suspects?"

Inspector Llorente's eyes met hers, a glint of something unreadable within their depths. "We're looking into several possibilities. It's too early to draw conclusions, but I assure you, we will get to the bottom of this. In the meantime, if you think of anything or anyone that might help our investigation, please don't hesitate to contact me."

"I will," Mia promised, a new resolve settling over her. She would find out what happened to Esteban, not just for her peace of mind, but for justice. As the inspector left, she turned back to her studio, the chaotic colors of her paintings now seeming like a map—complex and intricate, leading her to truths yet uncovered.

As the night deepened, Mia knew that the shadows cast by her doubts were just the beginning. She would need to navigate through the murkier waters of suspicion and betrayal, each revelation a stroke of clarity in the dark canvas of this mystery.

# Chapter 5: A Gathering of Shadows

As the morning sun painted the ancient cobblestones of Barcelona with hues of gold and amber, Mia found herself in a café not far from her studio, a rendezvous point chosen with deliberate intent. The day called for a meeting—a gathering of individuals who were not just familiar with Esteban's world, but who were also part of the intricate tapestry of his last days.

Mia watched as one by one, the invitees entered the café. Each was a character with their own brushstrokes upon the canvas of Esteban's life, and perhaps, upon the circumstances of his untimely demise.

First to arrive was Alba Gómez, a fiery art critic known for her sharp tongue and sharper pen. Her articles could make or break an exhibition, and her recent critiques had savaged more than one of Esteban's choices. Her presence was a stark reminder that words could carry motives as deadly as actions.

Next was Leon Delgado, a rival gallery owner whose competition with Esteban had often bordered on the vitriolic. His slicked-back hair and tailored suit did little to hide the hungry gleam in his eyes, a look that spoke of battles fought in the shadows of the art world.

Following Leon was Diego Torres, a young and ambitious artist whose career had skyrocketed after Esteban had controversially chosen to exclude him from a major exhibition. His inclusion in this circle was a nod to the enemies Esteban had made, his youthful arrogance masking an undercurrent of resentment.

The fourth to join was Lucia Marín, a collector whose wealth and influence were eclipsed only by her enigmatic aura. Her acquisitions often dictated market trends, and her recent transactions with Esteban had been the subject of hushed speculation. Her motives, like her expressions, remained unreadable.

Lastly, there was Isabella Castillo, a soft-spoken insurance broker specializing in art. Her last dealings with Esteban had been fraught with tension over a disputed valuation, a professional disagreement that hinted at deeper discord.

Mia greeted each guest as they arrived, her mind racing to piece together the puzzle each represented. The café buzzed with the murmur of other patrons, a soothing backdrop to the undercurrent of tension at their table.

Once they were all seated, Mia took a deep breath and began. "Thank you all for coming. As you know, we're all connected through Esteban... and his tragic passing has left many questions unanswered."

Alba leaned forward, her eyes sharp. "Are you suggesting one of us had a hand in his death, Mia?"

Before Mia could respond, Leon interjected, "That's a serious accusation to make without evidence."

Mia raised her hands, seeking to temper the rising heat. "I'm not accusing anyone. I just know that Esteban's death wasn't as straightforward as it seemed. And Inspector Llorente believes it was no accident."

The table fell into a stunned silence, broken only by Diego's scoff. "So, the great Esteban was pushed? Sounds like a plot from one of your abstract paintings, Mia."

Lucia's voice, when she spoke, was calm but icy. "Let's assume, for a moment, that it was not an accident. We are all here because we had some connection, some possible motive. But suspicion does not equal guilt."

Isabella, quiet until now, nodded slowly. "Exactly. And let's not forget the financial implications. Esteban's death could have triggered significant insurance claims, claims that I processed based on thorough assessments."

As accusations and defenses spiraled around the table, Mia felt the weight of the task ahead. Each of these individuals held a piece of the puzzle, and it was her job to assemble it—a daunting task, akin to discerning the subtle nuances of a complex painting.

But amidst the verbal parrying and guarded glances, Mia's attention kept returning to Leon. His animosity towards Esteban had been palpable, and his sudden eagerness to divert suspicion only deepened her misgivings.

As the meeting adjourned with no clear resolutions, Mia watched as the group dispersed, each person retreating behind their masks of civility. The morning's revelations had only deepened the shadows, and as she left the café, Mia knew that uncovering the truth in this labyrinth of motives and malice would require her to delve into the darkest corners of the art world—and of the human heart.

# Chapter 6: Tangled Lines

As dusk settled over Barcelona, casting a romantic hue across the bustling streets, Mia found herself in an increasingly complex emotional web. The investigation into Esteban's death had not only drawn her into a murky pool of suspicion and intrigue but also into an unforeseen tangle of personal attachments.

She had agreed to meet Inspector Llorente at a quiet, dimly lit bar near her studio, a place where the clink of glasses underscored hushed conversations. The inspector was already there, seated in a secluded corner, his presence somehow both reassuring and unsettling.

"Miss Valdés," he greeted, standing as she approached, his manners impeccably polite yet distinctly reserved.

"Inspector," Mia responded, her voice steadier than she felt. As she took her seat, the soft lighting of the bar illuminated Llorente's features in a way that softened the usual sternness of his expression.

"I wanted to discuss some developments in the case," he began, his eyes locking onto hers with an intensity that made her heart flutter unexpectedly. "But I must admit, part of me was also looking forward to seeing you again, outside the formalities of our investigation."

Mia's pulse quickened, her mind racing as she processed his words. Was it the gravity of the case that drew her to him, or something deeper, more personal?

Before she could respond, her phone vibrated insistently in her purse. It was Javier, his timing as if scripted to remind her of the complexities of her current life. "Excuse me, I need to take this," she said, stepping away to answer.

"Hey, are you still at the studio?" Javier's voice was tight, a note of concern threading through.

"No, I'm... out, discussing the case," Mia replied, careful not to divulge too much.

"I was hoping to see you tonight. There's something important we need to talk about," Javier pressed, his tone urgent.

"I'll be free later. Can it wait till then?" Mia asked, her gaze drifting back to Llorente, who was watching her with an unreadable expression.

"Alright, I'll wait at your place," Javier said, a hint of resignation in his voice.

Returning to the table, Mia found herself more aware of Llorente's magnetic presence. "Sorry about that," she murmured, trying to refocus on the reason for their meeting.

"No need to apologize," Llorente said, his voice low. "We all have our complexities."

The conversation slowly shifted back to the case, but the undercurrent of personal interest remained, palpable between them. Llorente shared his findings, his theories weaving through the facts like a skilled artist blending colors on a canvas. Yet, it was his subtle glances, the occasional lingering touch on her hand when passing a document, that spoke volumes beyond the spoken word.

As the meeting drew to a close, Mia felt torn. The inspector's charm was undeniable, and his intellectual allure was a strong contrast to Javier's more straightforward, passionate demeanor.

Stepping out into the cool night air, Mia's mind replayed the evening's exchanges. The love she felt for Javier was real and filled with history and shared dreams, but her interactions with Llorente stirred something different in her—a curious blend of intrigue and attraction that was both exhilarating and disconcerting.

As she made her way back to her apartment where Javier awaited, Mia knew she was walking into more than just a late-night discussion. She was stepping into a chapter of her life where the lines between love and duty, trust and suspicion, were as intertwined and complex as the plots of the novels she so loved to read. The coming conversation with Javier would not just be about their future, but also about how she navigated the intricate web of her feelings—a delicate balance between the safety of the known and the allure of the unknown.

# Chapter 7: Shadows and Loss

The night was unusually still as Mia approached her apartment. The usual cacophony of Barcelona's nightlife seemed muted, as if the city itself was holding its breath. Upon entering her home, she found Javier pacing the living room, a storm of worry etched across his face.

"Mia, thank God you're here," Javier rushed to her, his embrace a mix of relief and urgency. "I have something terrible to tell you—your studio, it's been burglarized."

Mia's heart sank. "What? When? How did you find out?"

"Just now," Javier replied, his voice tight with frustration. "I was on my way here when I decided to stop by your studio to check on some of the pieces for the exhibition. The door was ajar, and it looked like a hurricane had gone through the place."

The blood drained from Mia's face. Her studio was not just her workplace but her sanctuary. The thought of it being violated, her paintings possibly stolen or destroyed, was unbearable. "Did you call the police?"

"Yes, they're on their way there now. I came to get you first. I didn't want you to be alone when you saw it."

Grateful for his thoughtfulness yet reeling from the shock, Mia allowed herself a moment to gather her strength, then with Javier's supportive arm around her shoulders, they headed back to the studio.

The scene that greeted them was worse than Mia had feared. Canvases were slashed, paint jars shattered, and her tools scattered haphazardly around the room. Amid the chaos, it was clear that several valuable items were missing, including some rare vintage paints and a couple of her early works which had sentimental value.

As they waited for the police to arrive, Javier's previous warmth seemed to return as he stood protectively close, his earlier questions and suspicions temporarily forgotten in the face of Mia's distress. "Who could have done this?" Mia murmured, her voice barely a whisper as she took in the extent of the devastation.

"It's hard to say," Javier said, looking around with a furrowed brow. "This looks personal, Mia. It's not just a random act of vandalism; it's targeted."

The arrival of Inspector Llorente interrupted their somber assessment. His expression was one of professional concern as he surveyed the damage. "Miss Valdés, I'm terribly sorry to see this. We will do everything we can to find out who is responsible."

His words were reassuring, yet Mia couldn't shake off a nagging suspicion. The timing of the robbery—so soon after the revelation of Esteban's murder—seemed more than coincidental. It hinted at a deeper, more sinister connection, perhaps aimed at intimidating her or throwing her off track.

As Llorente and his team began their investigation, dusting for fingerprints and collecting evidence, Mia turned to Javier. "Do you think this could be related to Esteban's death?"

"It's possible," Javier admitted. "Whoever did this might be trying to scare you away from digging deeper."

The idea that her pursuit of truth might have provoked such a violent response was chilling. Yet, it only strengthened Mia's resolve to uncover the hidden facets of Esteban's life and death. If someone was desperate enough to invade her personal space, then she was undeniably close to uncovering something crucial.

Llorente approached them again, notebook in hand. "We'll need a list of anyone who might have had access to your studio, and anyone you suspect might bear a grudge."

Mia nodded, her mind already compiling names and faces, her artist's intuition blending with the nascent instincts of a detective. "I'll get that to you as soon as I can."

As the inspector walked away, Mia stood amidst the ruins of her creative space, her resolve hardening. The robbery was a message, but instead of instilling fear, it had ignited a fiercer determination. Whoever was behind this, and whatever their motives, Mia was more committed than ever to drawing them out of the shadows, into the stark light of justice.

# Chapter 8: Clues in the Chaos

The morning after the robbery was a grim affair. The sunlight that usually bathed Mia's studio in warmth now only highlighted the disarray left by the intruders. With the police having finished their preliminary investigation, Mia was left to sift through the remnants of her disrupted sanctuary.

Inspector Llorente had been thorough, leaving markers and notes indicating where evidence had been collected. Mia, despite the chaos, felt a surge of appreciation for the meticulous nature of his work, reflecting her own approach to art. Yet, as she began the arduous task of sorting through her scattered belongings, her mind couldn't help but wander to the enigma of Esteban's death and the possible connections to this brazen act of vandalism.

Among the strewn papers and broken frames, Mia stumbled upon a small, overlooked detail—a set of faint, muddy footprints leading to a corner of the studio that the thieves had seemingly ignored. Her pulse quickened. The police had missed this in their sweep, perhaps assuming the prints were old or irrelevant.

Armed with her phone, she snapped several pictures of the footprints before carefully covering them with sheets of paper to preserve what could be a crucial piece of evidence. This could be the break she needed, a tangible link to whoever was responsible not only for the robbery but possibly for what happened to Esteban.

As she continued her investigation, her phone rang. It was Javier, his voice filled with concern. "How are you holding up? I've been worried about you all morning."

Mia managed a weak smile, touched by his concern. "I'm okay, Javier. Actually, I might have found something the police missed. Can you come over?"

"Of course, I'll be there soon," he replied, the relief evident in his tone.

When Javier arrived, Mia showed him the concealed footprints. His eyes widened in surprise. "You think the thief made these?"

"It's possible," Mia mused. "And if we can match these prints to someone..."

They decided to keep this discovery between them until they could learn more. The last thing Mia needed was for potential suspects to know she was on their trail.

The next step was to revisit the list of people who had access to her studio. As she and Javier pored over the names, Mia couldn't shake off the feeling that the answer was hidden in plain sight, obscured by her proximity to the events and the people involved.

Later that day, Mia received a call from Lucia Marín, the enigmatic art collector. "Mia, I heard about the break-in. I'm so sorry. Is there anything I can do to help?"

Mia hesitated, then decided to take a chance. "Actually, Lucia, could we meet? I have something important to discuss, perhaps over coffee?"

"Of course, my dear. How about the café near the Plaza Real in an hour?"

"Perfect, see you then," Mia replied, her mind racing. Lucia had always been a puzzle, her motivations as layered and complex as any of Mia's paintings. If anyone had deeper insights into Esteban's dealings, it would be her.

At the café, Lucia greeted Mia with a warm, if somewhat calculating, smile. As they settled down with their coffees, Mia decided to be direct. "Lucia, you were close to Esteban. Did he ever mention any concerns about his safety or anyone he might have been worried about?"

Lucia's expression turned contemplative, her eyes narrowing slightly. "Esteban was a private man, but he did mention some tensions over certain dealings. He never gave specifics, but I could tell he was troubled."

Mia leaned in, her voice low. "Do you think someone could have wanted to hurt him because of those dealings?"

"It's possible," Lucia admitted, her tone serious. "In our world, art can be as much a curse as a blessing. It attracts all sorts of people, not all with good intentions."

As Mia absorbed her words, she realized that each conversation, each clue was like a brushstroke on a canvas, slowly revealing the larger picture. She thanked Lucia and left the café with a new sense of purpose. The puzzle was complex, but piece by piece, it was coming together, and Mia was determined to solve it, not just for Esteban's sake, but for her own peace of mind.

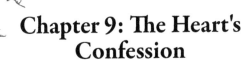

# Chapter 9: The Heart's Confession

As the Spanish sun cast long shadows over Barcelona's labyrinthine streets, Mia's thoughts tangled further, weaving a complex tapestry of suspicion and emotion. Her connection with Javier had always been a beacon of stability, yet the growing allure of Inspector Llorente's enigmatic presence introduced an unsettling yet thrilling dynamic to her life.

The studio was quiet, the usual hum of creativity stifled by the recent chaos. Javier had come to help Mia reorganize and restore some semblance of order, but the air between them was charged with an unspoken tension. Every glance and touch lingered a little longer than necessary, suggesting words left unsaid.

"Mia, about the other night at the bar with Llorente..." Javier began, breaking the silence as he moved a canvas. His voice was hesitant, probing the fragile peace that had settled between them.

Mia paused, her hands still on a paintbrush. She knew this conversation was inevitable. "Yes?"

"I couldn't help noticing... there's something different about how you are around him. It's like he sees a side of you that..." Javier's voice trailed off, his struggle to articulate his feelings evident.

Mia set down her brush, turning to face him fully. "Javier, Inspector Llorente and I are just working together. He's part of this whole situation with Esteban's death. That's all there is to it."

But even as she spoke, Mia knew her words skirted the edges of truth. Llorente did stir something in her, a part of her spirit that resonated with his intellectual curiosity and his solemn dedication.

"Mia, I know you, and it's more than just professional. Please, just be honest with me," Javier pleaded, his eyes searching hers for the truth.

Mia sighed, feeling the weight of the moment. "Javier, I won't lie to you. There is a certain... connection with him. It's different from what we have. It doesn't change how I feel about you, but it's there, and I can't ignore it."

Javier's expression darkened, a mix of hurt and understanding passing over his features. "I appreciate your honesty, Mia. I guess it's just hard to hear. I love you, and the thought of losing you to this—or to him—it scares me."

The vulnerability in his voice tugged at Mia's heart. She reached out, taking his hands in hers. "Javier, you've always been my rock. This situation with Esteban, the robbery, it's thrown me into a world of uncertainty. Llorente is a part of that world, but you, you're my home."

Javier nodded slowly, squeezing her hands. "I just want to make sure we're on the same page, Mia. We've been through so much together. I don't want to lose what we have."

As they resumed their task, the tension slowly dissipated, replaced by a renewed sense of understanding. However, the emotional clarity was short-lived.

Later that evening, Inspector Llorente called. "Miss Valdés, could we meet tomorrow? There are some developments in the case I need to discuss with you privately."

Mia agreed, feeling a surge of both professional necessity and personal curiosity. As she hung up, she realized that her feelings for Llorente were complicating her life in ways she hadn't anticipated.

The next morning, as Mia prepared for her meeting, she felt a duality within her—a conflict between the comforting love she felt for Javier and the intellectually charged connection with Llorente. This meeting would not just be a discussion about the case but also a test of her own emotions and choices.

As she stepped out into the crisp morning air, Mia knew that the choices she made now would shape not only the investigation but also the landscape of her heart. With each step towards the café where Llorente awaited, she felt like a character in one of her beloved mystery novels, where every chapter held a clue, and every decision could unravel either truth or consequence.

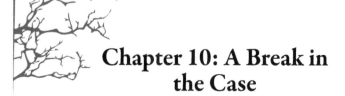

# Chapter 10: A Break in the Case

M ia walked into the quaint café, her heart aflutter with a cocktail of anticipation and trepidation. Inspector Llorente was already there, seated at a secluded table that offered a panoramic view of the bustling street outside. His posture was relaxed, but his eyes, sharp and discerning, acknowledged her the moment she stepped through the door.

"Miss Valdés," he greeted, standing briefly as she approached. His manners were impeccable, a trait that Mia found increasingly endearing.

"Inspector Llorente," Mia replied, settling into the chair opposite him. The café's ambiance was a blend of old-world charm and modern bustle, a fitting backdrop for the conversation they were about to have.

"I've brought you here because we've made significant progress in the investigation," Llorente began, his voice low and steady. He slid a folder across the table towards her. "After examining the evidence you found—those footprints in your studio—we were able to make a match."

Mia's eyes widened as she opened the folder. Inside were photographs of the footprints alongside comparison prints taken from a suspect. "These belong to Leon Delgado," Llorente explained. "It appears that your intuition about someone with a personal vendetta was correct."

Leon Delgado, the rival gallery owner with a history of bitter competition with Esteban, had been on her list of suspects, but seeing the evidence laid out so concretely was still a shock. "How did you find him?"

"We revisited the list of individuals who had recent conflicts with Esteban," Llorente continued. "After you discovered the footprints, we obtained a warrant to search Delgado's home and gallery. We found a pair of shoes that matched the prints exactly. We also uncovered several items that were missing from your studio."

Mia felt a mix of relief and anxiety churn within her. The case was moving forward, yet the implications were enormous. "What happens now?"

"Delgado is in custody and will be questioned. We believe he may also have information about Esteban's death," Llorente said. His gaze lingered on Mia, a softening in his eyes. "Your help has been invaluable, Mia. I must admit, your involvement has brought a new dimension to this case."

The compliment stirred something within Mia, a sense of professional pride mingled with the personal connection that had been slowly, yet inexorably, developing between them. "Thank you, Inspector. I just want to see justice done."

"As do I," Llorente affirmed. He then shifted slightly, leaning closer. "Mia, if I may be so bold, it's not just the case that has captured my interest. I find your insight, your dedication... quite remarkable."

Mia felt her cheeks warm under his gaze. The burgeoning feelings she had been wrestling with seemed to crystallize in that moment, a clear and present dilemma between her longstanding relationship with Javier and the compelling new bond forming with Llorente.

"Inspector, I—" Mia began, then paused, unsure of how to continue.

"Please, call me Carlos," he interjected softly.

"Carlos," she repeated, the name feeling both foreign and familiar on her lips. "I appreciate your words, and I'd be lying if I said I haven't felt... something. But this is complicated. There's a lot at stake, and I have a lot to consider."

Llorente nodded, his expression understanding. "Of course, Mia. I would never ask you to make decisions lightly. Just know that whatever happens, I have the utmost respect for you."

Their conversation drifted back to the case, but the undercurrents of their personal discourse remained, an uncharted territory that both intrigued and intimidated Mia.

As she left the café, the dossier under her arm felt heavier than mere paper. It carried the weight of the unfolding case and the burgeoning emotional entanglements that accompanied it. The road ahead was fraught with legal and ethical dilemmas, but also with personal choices that Mia knew would define the contours of her heart and life.

# Chapter 11: Revelations and Doubts

As the late afternoon sun dipped behind the gothic silhouettes of Barcelona's architecture, casting elongated shadows across the cobblestone streets, Mia sat alone in her somewhat restored studio. The walls, lined with her vibrant canvases, seemed to echo the tumult within her mind—a mixture of relief, suspicion, and unresolved emotions.

The breakthrough in the case had brought a degree of solace. Leon Delgado being linked to the robbery at her studio meant a part of the mystery was unraveling. However, the connection to Esteban's death still hung in the air, an unsolved puzzle that gnawed at her conscience. Mia couldn't shake off the feeling that the robbery and the murder were intertwined, pieces of a larger, more sinister plot.

Her thoughts were interrupted by a gentle knock on the door. It was Javier, his face a mask of concern and tentative smiles. "How are you holding up?" he asked as he stepped inside, his eyes quickly scanning the still-disheveled corners of the studio.

"I'm managing," Mia replied, forcing a small smile. "We've made some progress on the case. It turns out Leon Delgado was behind the robbery."

Javier's eyebrows rose in surprise. "Delgado? That doesn't surprise me, but it's good to have confirmation. And what about Esteban's case? Any leads there?"

"They're still investigating. It's complicated, and there's a lot they haven't pieced together yet," Mia responded, her voice trailing off as she turned to face a partially covered canvas, its colors clashing violently—a mirror to her inner turmoil.

Javier moved closer, his presence comforting yet charged with an unspoken question. "And how are you and Llorente getting along? I mean, in the investigation?" His attempt to sound casual was betrayed by a barely perceptible tension in his voice.

Mia sighed, knowing the complexity of her feelings for Llorente couldn't be easily explained or dismissed. "He's been professional. Very thorough. He... respects my input," she answered carefully, her eyes still fixed on the chaotic swirls of paint before her.

Javier nodded, his gaze lingering on her profile. "Mia, I know this isn't just about the case for you. I see how he looks at you, and I can't help but feel..." He paused, struggling to find the right words, "...that I might lose you to whatever this is becoming."

Mia turned to face him, her heart aching at the pain in his eyes. "Javier, you are incredibly important to me. Nothing has changed that. But I need to follow this through, not just the case but understanding what I feel. I owe you honesty—it's confusing, and I'm trying to figure it out."

Javier reached out to gently touch her arm, his gesture one of unconditional support. "I get it, Mia. And I'm here, no matter how complex it gets. Just... don't lose yourself in this chaos."

The conversation left Mia more unsettled. She knew Javier's fears weren't unfounded. Her growing connection with Llorente was undeniable, yet she wasn't ready to explore the depths of those feelings, not while a murder investigation loomed over them all.

Later that evening, after Javier had left, Mia received a call from Inspector Llorente. His voice was urgent, a stark contrast to his usual composed demeanor. "Mia, can you meet me tomorrow morning? There's been a development—something we didn't see coming. It's about Esteban's case."

"Of course, I'll be there," Mia replied, her pulse quickening with both anticipation and dread.

As she hung up the phone, the studio seemed to close in around her, the shadows of the evening mingling with the shadows in her heart. The truth was close, she could feel it. But with the truth came the inevitable unraveling of many threads, some of which Mia feared might lead back to her own door. As she prepared for the night, Mia knew the coming day would bring answers that would change everything—not just the mystery of Esteban's death, but the very fabric of her own life.

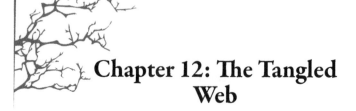

# Chapter 12: The Tangled Web

Mia arrived at the quaint café early the next morning, her mind a whirlpool of thoughts and theories about the call from Inspector Llorente. The early hours found the streets of Barcelona still cloaked in the remnants of night, with only the faint murmur of the city awakening. The café, a usual spot for such clandestine meetings, seemed more like a stage set for revelations that could very well tilt her world.

She spotted Llorente already at a table, his posture betraying an urgency that was unusual for the composed inspector. As Mia approached, he stood, greeting her with a nod that conveyed both respect and the gravity of the situation.

"Thank you for coming, Miss Valdés," he began, motioning for her to sit. "What I'm about to share must stay between us until we can verify all the facts."

Mia nodded, her heart rate picking up. "Of course, Inspector."

Llorente took a deep breath, his usual reserve giving way to a slight edge of concern. "We received a tip-off last night. It seems there might be more to Esteban's dealings than we initially suspected. The robbery at your studio might have been a diversion."

"A diversion?" Mia echoed, confusion and intrigue knitting her brow.

"Yes," Llorente continued. "Our informant suggests that Esteban was about to expose a major forgery ring within the art community here in Barcelona. It seems he stumbled upon this quite by accident, and it may have cost him his life."

Mia's thoughts raced. Esteban's passion for authenticity in art was well-known, and his disdain for forgeries was almost a crusade. "Do you think this ring targeted him to prevent being exposed?"

"It's highly probable," Llorente said, his eyes scanning the café before returning to Mia. "And there's more. The informant linked one name to the ring that you might know—Lucia Marín."

Mia felt as though the floor had dropped from beneath her. Lucia, with her extensive art collection and her inscrutable manner, had always seemed above reproach. "Lucia? But how—why would she?"

"It appears her collection isn't as legitimate as we believed. Many pieces, which she passed off as originals, might be sophisticated forgeries," Llorente explained, his voice low and steady despite the shocking information.

The implications were staggering. If Lucia was involved, the depth of deceit was profound, and it painted a target on anyone who came too close to the truth. "What do you need from me?" Mia asked, her resolve hardening despite the shock.

"For now, keep this information to yourself. Continue as usual. We don't want to tip off Lucia or anyone else involved that we're on to them," Llorente instructed. "And be careful. If they suspected Esteban was onto them, they won't hesitate to come after anyone else poking around."

Mia nodded, the weight of the situation settling on her shoulders. As she left the café, the city seemed different to her—a façade hiding secrets that were darker than she had ever imagined.

The rest of the day passed in a blur. Mia found herself back at her studio, staring at her canvases, seeing not just colors and shapes but hidden messages and meanings that mirrored the duplicity in the art world she was now entangled with. Her thoughts kept drifting back to Lucia, to their last conversation, and to the chilling realization that the art collector's refined demeanor might have concealed a ruthless criminal mind.

That evening, as the sun set over Barcelona, painting the sky with strokes of crimson and gold, Mia knew that her next steps had to be calculated with precision. The forgery ring, Lucia's involvement, and the dangerous implications of her continued investigation loomed large, casting long shadows across her path.

The tangled web of deceit was unraveling, and Mia was at its very heart, playing a role she never envisioned—in a story where art and crime were indistinguishably blended, and where each brushstroke could be her last.

# Chapter 13: A Brush with Danger

The evening air was crisp as Mia walked briskly towards the gallery where Esteban had spent many of his final days. The gallery, usually a place of sanctuary and artistic celebration, now felt like a crime scene hiding in plain sight. The streets of Barcelona hummed with the usual nocturnal activities, but to Mia, every shadow seemed darker, every whisper a potential threat.

Her meeting with Lucia Marín was scheduled under the guise of discussing a potential acquisition. Mia's heart pounded with a mix of fear and determination as she approached the gallery's ornate entrance. The heavy wooden door swung open, revealing the dimly lit interior, where the walls were adorned with masterpieces that might hold secrets deeper than their brush strokes.

Lucia was already there, elegant as always in a flowing silk dress, her demeanor calm and collected. "Mia, darling, so good to see you," she greeted with a warm smile, though her eyes held a sharpness that hadn't been as pronounced before.

"Lucia, thank you for meeting me," Mia replied, managing a polite smile. "I've been thinking a lot about expanding my collection."

Lucia led her through the gallery, commenting on various pieces with expert knowledge and occasional anecdotes that highlighted her deep involvement in the art world. Mia listened, her mind racing, trying to reconcile this cultured woman with the criminal activities Llorente had described.

As they stopped before a particularly striking painting, Lucia's tone shifted subtly. "Mia, I must confess, it's refreshing to discuss art with someone who understands its true value, not just the price tag."

Mia nodded, her senses heightened. "Yes, the art's true value. Like ensuring its authenticity, right, Lucia?"

The slight pause was almost imperceptible. "Of course, authenticity is paramount," Lucia affirmed, her gaze fixed on Mia.

The conversation moved to a private viewing room. As Lucia poured two glasses of wine, Mia felt the walls closing in. She knew she was walking a tightrope. "Lucia, I've also been thinking about the history of pieces. After Esteban's tragic death, I've become more... concerned about the provenance of art."

Lucia handed her a glass, her hand steady. "Understandable. Esteban's death was a loss to all of us. He had such an eye for detail. Sometimes, I think it got him into trouble."

Mia's pulse quickened. "What kind of trouble?"

Lucia sipped her wine, her eyes narrowing slightly. "Let's just say, he was becoming quite interested in the origins of certain pieces. It's a pity he didn't have more time to explore his theories."

Realization dawned on Mia, the implications clear and chilling. Lucia wasn't just involved; she was deeply embedded in whatever Esteban had uncovered. Mia set down her glass, untouched. "Lucia, if there's anything you think I should know about—"

The sound of the door clicking shut interrupted her. Lucia's expression hardened. "Mia, you are a talented artist and a good friend. But I advise you not to delve into matters that don't concern you."

The threat was veiled but unmistakable. Mia stood, her own resolve firming. "I believe these matters concern anyone who values the integrity of art."

Lucia's smile was cold, a mask slipping back into place. "Be careful, Mia. The art world can be more cutthroat than you imagine."

With that, Lucia exited, leaving Mia alone amidst the curated beauty that now felt oppressive. As Mia left the gallery, the weight of her discovery lay heavy on her shoulders. She was more certain than ever that Lucia was at the heart of the forgery ring, and that uncovering the truth would put her in greater danger than she'd ever faced before.

The walk home was a blur of heightened senses and racing thoughts. Mia knew she had to tread carefully, playing a dangerous game against opponents who wouldn't hesitate to silence threats to their empire. As she reached her apartment, the safety of home never felt more like a sanctuary. Yet, the night's revelations had irrevocably changed the stakes, pushing Mia deeper into a mystery that was as dangerous as it was compelling.

# Chapter 14: The Veil Lifts

Mia spent a restless night, her dreams haunted by shadowy figures lurking in the background of her beloved canvases. Morning found her at her studio early, the familiar smell of oil paint and turpentine a comforting reminder of her real world, even as the undercurrents of deceit swirled around her.

She had barely set up her palette when Javier walked in, his face etched with concern. "Mia, you look like you didn't sleep. What's wrong?"

Mia hesitated, weighing the risk of involving Javier further but realizing she needed someone she could trust completely. "I met with Lucia Marín last night," she began, watching his reaction closely. "I think she's deeply involved in the forgery ring Inspector Llorente mentioned."

Javier's brow furrowed in worry. "That's serious, Mia. You need to be careful—people like that can be dangerous."

"I know," Mia sighed, her brush dipping into the blue absentmindedly. "She made it clear that I should stay away from investigating further."

"But you won't, will you?" Javier knew her too well.

Mia shook her head. "I can't. Not now. Not with Esteban's memory and the integrity of the art world at stake."

Javier nodded, his determination firming. "Then I'm with you, every step of the way. What's our next move?"

"We need more evidence. Something concrete to link Lucia directly to the forgeries and possibly to Esteban's death," Mia stated, setting down her brush and turning to face him.

As they plotted their course of action, Mia's phone rang. It was Inspector Llorente, his voice urgent. "Mia, can you come to the station? We've made a significant discovery."

At the station, Llorente led them to his office, where several pieces of artwork lay spread across his desk alongside documents and photographs. "We raided one of Lucia Marín's storage facilities early this morning," he explained, indicating the items on his desk. "We found multiple artworks with questionable provenance and several that are confirmed forgeries."

Mia approached the desk, her eyes scanning the forged pieces—brilliant in execution but soulless in essence. "These were all in Lucia's possession?"

"Yes, and we found correspondence that suggests she was planning to sell these at an upcoming auction," Llorente added, handing her a stack of emails printed out.

The emails were damning, filled with coded messages that correlated with incoming shipments of art supplies typically used for aging materials and altering artworks. "This is it, then. This could prove her involvement," Mia said, a mix of triumph and trepidation in her voice.

"We still need to link her directly to Esteban's death. For that, we need to know what he found out exactly that made him a target," Llorente pointed out.

Mia nodded, her mind working rapidly. "I'll go back to the gallery, see if I can access his personal records or anything he might have left behind that points to his discoveries."

"Be careful, Mia. She's already suspicious, and she won't hesitate to act if she feels threatened," Llorente warned, his concern evident.

Back at her studio, Mia prepared herself mentally and physically for what might be the most dangerous part of her investigation. As she sifted through her own collection of sketches and tools, she felt a resolve steeling within her. This was no longer just about her art—it was about justice, about preserving the sanctity of creative expression against those who would corrupt it for personal gain.

As the sun began to set, casting long shadows across her canvases, Mia steeled herself for the confrontation ahead. The truth was close, almost within reach, and she was determined to expose it, whatever the cost.

# Chapter 15: Unveiling the Truth

Armed with determination and a keen sense of justice, Mia made her way back to Esteban's gallery under the pretense of collecting some of her personal items that had been left there before his untimely demise. The gallery, usually a place brimming with life and the appreciation of art, now held a more sinister significance. It was not just a repository of beauty, but potentially a vault of secrets and lies.

Upon arrival, Mia was greeted by the gallery assistant, Tomas, a young man with a sincere passion for art that had always reminded her of her early days. "Mia, it's good to see you. I heard about the break-in at your studio. Are you okay?" Tomas asked, concern marking his youthful features.

"I'm fine, Tomas, thank you. I just need to pick up some things that Esteban had agreed to store for me," Mia replied, maintaining her composure despite the anxiety that gnawed at her.

"Of course, let me show you to the back. There's been a lot of sorting out since... well, since everything happened," Tomas said as he led her through the familiar corridors of the gallery.

Once in the storage room, Mia quickly scanned the area for any sign of Esteban's personal effects. She knew that finding anything directly linking Lucia to the forgeries or Esteban's death might be a long shot, but she had to start somewhere.

"Actually, Tomas, did Esteban keep any personal records here? Maybe files or notes?" Mia asked, trying to sound casual.

Tomas nodded, pointing to a filing cabinet in the corner. "Yeah, he kept some records and personal notes in there. He was always scribbling down thoughts and ideas. Said it helped him keep his thoughts organized."

Mia's heart raced as she approached the cabinet. Pulling open the drawers, she rifled through files and papers, her fingers searching for anything out of the ordinary. Then, tucked between auction catalogs and artist bios, she found a small, nondescript notebook.

Flipping through it, Mia discovered it was more than just a repository of thoughts; it was Esteban's ledger of suspicions. In his meticulous handwriting, he had noted discrepancies in several transactions that had not seemed important at the time but now appeared to be coded references to the forgeries. His last entries were frantic, more disjointed, indicating he was onto something big—something dangerous.

As Mia absorbed the information, her skin prickled with the realization of how much danger Esteban must have been in. She carefully tucked the notebook into her bag, her resolve hardening. This was the evidence they needed, but it also made her a target.

"Tomas, I found what I was looking for. Thanks for letting me look around," Mia said, her voice steady despite the storm of emotions inside her.

"Anytime, Mia. Take care, okay?" Tomas replied, his smile faintly masking his concern.

Leaving the gallery, Mia felt the weight of the notebook against her side—a weight not of its physical heft, but of its potential to bring justice for Esteban and cleanse the art community of its hidden rot.

Her next stop was the police station, where she planned to deliver the notebook to Inspector Llorente. However, as she walked the familiar route, a prickling sense of being watched crept over her. Turning suddenly, she caught a fleeting glimpse of a figure darting into the shadows.

Mia's heart pounded as she quickened her pace, the dangers Esteban faced now starkly real and immediate in her own life. She was close to unveiling the truth, but the closer she got, the more perilous her path became. As she neared the safety of the police station, Mia knew the final confrontation was inevitable, and she braced herself for the challenges ahead. The endgame was in sight, and she was ready to face it, no matter the cost.

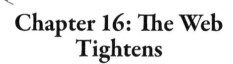

# Chapter 16: The Web Tightens

As Mia hurried through the brisk evening, her thoughts churned with the revelations found in Esteban's notebook. The evidence within those pages was more than incriminating; it was a map of hidden connections and dark transactions that painted a disturbing picture of the art world she loved so dearly. Each step towards the police station made her heart beat faster, not just from fear, but from the burden of carrying a truth that was both liberating and dangerous.

Upon reaching the police station, Mia was ushered quickly into Inspector Llorente's office. The gravity of the situation was mirrored in his expression as he greeted her. "Mia, you look troubled. What have you found?"

Mia wasted no time, pulling out the notebook and placing it on his desk. "Esteban's notes. They're more than just random thoughts. They're observations, suspicions about forgeries, about artists being more involved than just creating. It connects a lot of dots, particularly around Lucia Marín."

Llorente flipped through the notebook, his brows knitting together as he scanned the entries. "This could be the break we need to tie everything together. Good work, Mia."

Despite the praise, Mia felt a knot of anxiety tighten in her stomach. "Carlos, I think I was followed here."

His attention snapped up from the pages. "Followed? Did you see who it was?"

"Not clearly. Just a figure slipping into the shadows. But it's clear that someone knows I'm digging into this too deeply," Mia replied, her voice tinged with worry.

Llorente's eyes darkened with concern. "We need to take extra precautions then. I can arrange for surveillance on your studio and home, at least until we sort this out."

Mia nodded, grateful for the protection but uneasy about the level of danger she now found herself in. "Thank you, Carlos. I just want this to be over."

"We're close, Mia. This notebook is a substantial piece of evidence. I'll have my team work on corroborating the details as quickly as possible," Llorente assured her, but his tone carried the weight of the task ahead.

As Mia left the police station, the reality of her situation settled in. She was pivotal in uncovering a major criminal enterprise, and now she was a target. The walk home was filled with over-the-shoulder glances and jumps at every shadow. Arriving home, she double-checked every lock and window, a new routine that underscored her fear.

Later that night, as Mia sat in her living room surrounded by her own artwork, she pondered the strange twist her life had taken. From artist to amateur detective, her journey was something out of one of the mystery novels she read for inspiration—not something she ever imagined living through. Every sound in her apartment made her heart skip, every shadow through her curtains made her flinch. The solitude of her studio, once her sanctuary, now felt isolating and vulnerable.

Her phone buzzed, a message from Javier: "Just checking in, how are you holding up?"

Mia typed back a brief response, trying not to let her worry show. "Got some leads. Can't wait for this to be over."

Javier's reply was immediate and comforting. "Hang in there. I'm here for anything you need."

Closing her eyes, Mia tried to envision a return to normalcy, to days focused on palettes and textures rather than suspects and motives. But first, she had to see this through, no matter how dangerous the path became. With each piece of the puzzle falling into place, her resolve hardened. She would see justice done for Esteban and ensure the art world was cleansed of its corrupt elements. But at what cost to her peace of mind and safety? Only time would tell.

# Chapter 17: A Dangerous Game

Mia awoke the next morning to the dull hum of anxiety that had become her constant companion. Today, she knew, would be critical. With the evidence compiled and Esteban's notes securely in the hands of Inspector Llorente, the investigation was reaching a crescendo. The anticipation of confrontation with those implicated was palpable.

As she prepared for the day, Mia's thoughts were interrupted by a call from Inspector Llorente. "Mia, we need you to come to the station. We're planning our next moves, and your insights could be crucial."

Arriving at the station, Mia found Llorente and his team gathered around a large table littered with photographs, documents, and notes. The atmosphere was charged, each officer acutely aware of the stakes involved.

"Thank you for coming," Llorente said, gesturing to a seat. "We've verified several of Esteban's observations from the notebook. It's as we feared—the forgery ring is extensive, and it's deeply embedded in the local art scene."

Mia took her seat, her resolve strengthening despite her nerves. "What's the plan?"

"We're going to conduct a series of raids," Llorente explained. "We believe we've located the workshops where the forgeries are made. We also have enough to bring Lucia Marín in for questioning. Your testimony could be pivotal in tying her statements to discrepancies we've found."

The mention of facing Lucia directly sent a shiver down Mia's spine, but she nodded in agreement. "I'll do whatever it takes to see justice served."

Llorente gave a grim smile. "We appreciate your courage. We'll have officers with you at all times for your safety."

The day progressed in a flurry of activity. Mia watched as plans were drawn up, routes confirmed, and backup prepared. It was like witnessing a strategic battle being orchestrated, with the gallery as the fortress to be besieged.

Late in the afternoon, just as the sun began to cast long shadows over the city, the operation commenced. Mia was in a police car with Llorente and a small convoy of other units as they approached Lucia's gallery. Her heart raced as they parked discreetly around the corner.

"Stay here until I give the signal," Llorente instructed, his expression tense as he checked his weapon and prepared to move out.

Mia watched as the team, with practiced precision, moved towards the gallery. The minutes stretched into what seemed hours, each second ticking by with excruciating slowness. Then, the radio crackled to life, and Llorente's voice confirmed, "We're in. Suspect is secured. No injuries."

Relief flooded Mia, followed quickly by a surge of adrenaline. "Can I see her?" she asked, her voice steady.

"Soon. Let's go."

Inside the gallery, Mia was met with the sight of Lucia Marín, handcuffed but defiant, surrounded by officers. Her gaze met Mia's, a mix of betrayal and resignation flashing across her features.

"Mia, why?" Lucia's voice was a low hiss.

"You were my mentor, Lucia," Mia replied, her voice calm but firm. "You taught me to value the truth in art. This—what you've done—it's a betrayal of everything art stands for."

As Lucia was led away, Mia felt a chapter close on a painful part of her life. But the game was not over yet. There were still pieces to be placed, and Mia knew her role in this saga would continue until every thread of deceit was unraveled.

Returning to the station, Mia felt a mixture of triumph and weariness. The battle was won, but the war against corruption in the art world still loomed large. As she helped Llorente and his team prepare for the trials and further investigations, Mia knew her journey through the shadows of the art world was far from over. But with each step, she was restoring integrity to the field she loved, ensuring that beauty and truth remained at the heart of art.

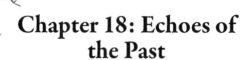

# Chapter 18: Echoes of the Past

T he gallery was quiet, the usual hum of visitor chatter and footsteps silenced by the recent events. Mia walked through the now empty halls, each artwork hanging solemnly as if mourning the disgrace of its custodians. The successful raid and Lucia's arrest had sent shockwaves through the local art community, revealing the extent of the corruption that had hidden beneath the polished veneer of cultured respectability.

Mia's role in uncovering the forgery ring had not gone unnoticed. While many hailed her bravery, others whispered of betrayal, not yet understanding the necessity of her actions. Today, she was back in the gallery, not as an artist or a detective, but as a witness to the cleanup operation. The police had asked her to identify any pieces she could confirm as forgeries, a task that was both heartbreaking and cathartic.

Inspector Llorente joined her as she examined a particularly striking piece, a supposed original that she had admired countless times before. "It's a fake," Mia said, her voice tinged with sadness. "The brushwork is all wrong, and the palette is too bright for the era it's supposed to represent."

Llorente nodded, making notes on his clipboard. "Your expertise has been invaluable, Mia. Without your eye for detail, we might have missed these."

As they moved through the gallery, Mia reflected on the past weeks. The investigation had taken a toll on her, both emotionally and physically. The gallery that had once been a place of inspiration was now a crime scene, a reminder of the betrayal of one of her mentors.

"I never thought the art world I loved could be so... corrupt," Mia confessed as they paused before another forged masterpiece.

"It's not just the art world," Llorente replied. "Anywhere there's money and prestige, there's the potential for corruption. But there's also always someone willing to stand up for what's right. You did that, Mia."

Mia smiled weakly, appreciating his support. "What happens now?"

"We build the case for trial. With Lucia in custody and the evidence we've collected, it's a strong case. But there will be more to do—tracking down other members of the ring, ensuring this doesn't happen again," Llorente explained.

"And the gallery?" Mia glanced around at the empty walls and the few remaining artworks not marked for confiscation.

"It will remain closed for the time being. The ownership will likely revert to a state trust until it can be determined how to proceed. And we'll need to review all acquisitions made during Lucia's tenure," Llorente detailed the road ahead.

Mia nodded, understanding the necessity of each step. "I'd like to help with that. To restore some integrity here."

"I was hoping you'd say that," Llorente smiled. "Your involvement could make a big difference."

As they left the gallery, Mia felt a chapter closing behind her. The road ahead would be challenging, but necessary to heal the wounds inflicted upon the art community.

Back at her studio, Mia resumed her own work, her canvases now reflecting a mixture of sorrow and hope. The experience had changed her, deepening her understanding of her craft and of human nature. As she painted, she thought of Esteban, hoping that her actions had honored his memory and what he had stood for.

The evening light faded into twilight as Mia added the final touches to a piece inspired by the events she had lived through. It was a complex blend of dark and light, truth and deception, mirroring the journey she had undertaken.

In the quiet of her studio, surrounded by her art, Mia knew the fight for integrity was far from over. But she was ready for whatever came next, armed with her brushes, her integrity, and a newfound strength that no forger could ever replicate.

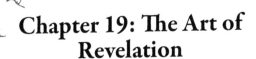

# Chapter 19: The Art of Revelation

Mia's days following the upheaval in the art community found her studio transformed into a sanctuary not only for herself but also for the truth. Her latest series of paintings, inspired by the dual themes of corruption and redemption, were beginning to take shape on the sprawling canvases that lined her studio walls.

As she mixed a palette of somber grays and vibrant golds, her phone rang, a gentle interruption in the quiet morning. It was Inspector Llorente, his voice carrying a tone of finality that immediately drew Mia's attention. "We've scheduled a press conference for tomorrow," he informed her. "We'll be announcing the charges against Lucia and others involved in the forgery ring. We would like you to be there, Mia, to speak about the impact of this case on the art community."

Mia hesitated, the weight of the request settling heavily on her shoulders. "I'll be there, Carlos. It's important that the community understands what happened and why."

"Thank you, Mia. Your voice carries a lot of weight now, not just as a victim but as a champion for authenticity," Llorente replied, a note of respect in his voice.

The next morning, as Mia stood behind the podium, facing a sea of reporters, her hands trembled slightly—not from fear, but from the responsibility of her words. She recounted the journey of the investigation, praising the diligent efforts of the police and condemning the greed that had tainted the sacred halls of art. "Art is not just an investment; it's a legacy of our culture, our emotions, and our humanity," Mia declared, her voice strengthening with each word.

As the flash of cameras and scribble of reporters' pens captured her statement, Mia felt a sense of closure. The story of corruption had been told, but so too had the story of resilience and integrity.

Following the conference, as Mia walked through the city, she felt the gazes of those who recognized her. Some were filled with gratitude, others with a new awareness of the vulnerability of their world.

Back at her studio, Mia received a visitor, a young artist named Elena, who had recently moved to Barcelona. "Ms. Valdés, I've followed your work, and especially your role in uncovering the forgery ring. I just wanted to say thank you, for standing up for all of us," Elena expressed earnestly.

Mia smiled, touched by Elena's words. "Thank you, Elena. It's important to remember that art should represent truth and beauty, not deceit."

Elena nodded, her eyes reflecting a mix of admiration and resolve. "I hope to learn from your strength and integrity."

As the young artist left, Mia returned to her canvas, her brush strokes reflecting a medley of the emotions she had experienced: betrayal, resolve, and ultimately, hope. The colors blended on the canvas, telling a story not just of a scandal that shook the city, but of a community that stood strong against adversity.

The evening drew to a close with Mia stepping back to view her completed series. Each piece told a part of the story, and together, they formed a narrative of triumph over corruption. Mia knew these pieces would resonate with viewers, not just as art, but as milestones in her own journey and that of the art community.

The trials and the public revelations had changed Mia, as they had changed the art scene in Barcelona. But as she cleaned her brushes and turned off the lights in her studio, she felt a peace that had eluded her since the investigation began. The truth had been a hard master, but it had also been a profound teacher.

Mia locked the studio door behind her, the click echoing softly in the quiet street. She walked home through the city she loved, a city that had shown her its darkest shadows and its brightest lights, knowing that her journey through art and truth was far from over, but ready for whatever came next.

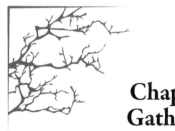

# Chapter 20: The Gathering Storm

The weeks following the press conference saw a whirlwind of activity within the art community of Barcelona. Galleries that had once lauded Lucia Marín's impeccable taste were now scrutinizing their collections, fearful of the taint of forgery. The cultural landscape was shifting, and at the center of this transformation was Mia, whose courage and integrity had sparked a city-wide reevaluation of art's true value.

Despite the praise and newfound respect, Mia found little time to rest. Her studio became a hub for discussions about art authenticity, hosting meetings with gallery owners, curators, and even policymakers who were intent on reforming how art was traded and valued. Her paintings, vibrant with the tumult of recent events, drew significant attention, symbolizing the resilience of truth in a world marred by deceit.

One rainy afternoon, as the city prepared for the upcoming storm, Mia received an unexpected visit from Inspector Llorente. His presence always signified seriousness, and today was no exception. "Mia, we've encountered something that might interest you," he began, shedding his coat and settling into the familiar comfort of Mia's studio. "In our ongoing investigations, we've uncovered a diary—Lucia's diary. It mentions you several times."

Mia's interest was piqued, a mix of apprehension and curiosity washing over her. "What does it say?"

"It seems she admired you greatly, at first," Llorente explained, pulling a small, leather-bound book from his bag. "She saw in you a kindred spirit of sorts. But as your mentor, Esteban, began his inquiries, her entries about you changed—she felt betrayed, thinking you might side with him against her if you knew the truth."

The revelation stung, the idea that Lucia had once respected her only to feel betrayed by Mia's unwitting role in the unfolding scandal. It added a layer of complexity to the narrative that Mia hadn't considered.

"Would you like to keep the diary?" Llorente offered, his eyes soft with sympathy.

Mia nodded, her hands slightly trembling as she accepted the diary. The weight of the book felt heavier than it looked, laden with the personal thoughts of a woman she had once admired and trusted.

As Llorente left, the storm broke over Barcelona, the rain tapping a steady rhythm against the studio windows. Mia opened the diary, the pages filled with elegant, flowing script that belied the turmoil of the author's soul. She read about Lucia's aspirations, her fears, and ultimately, her descent into the forgery ring that promised to protect her status at any cost.

The diary was not just a catalog of crimes; it was a mirror to the art world's often unseen pressures—the demand for continual success, the fear of obscurity, and the allure of easy solutions. Mia felt a sorrow for Lucia, a feeling tempered by the knowledge of the harm she had caused.

The next day, with the storm cleared and the city washed anew, Mia decided to host an exhibit, not just of her recent works but also featuring excerpts from Lucia's diary. She wanted to show the complexity of the human condition—the blending of ambition, fear, and the potential for redemption.

As the exhibit opened, the response was overwhelming. Visitors walked through the gallery, pausing at each painting and accompanying diary entry, reflecting on the stark revelations of each piece. Mia's work had always evoked emotion, but now it stirred a deeper contemplation about the ethics and responsibilities inherent in the creation and curation of art.

Standing amid her paintings, Mia felt the weight of her journey from artist to accidental detective to a vocal advocate for integrity in art. The path had been fraught with challenges, but it had led to a deeper understanding of her role not just as an artist, but as a guardian of culture.

As the exhibit drew to a close, Mia stood by the window, looking out over the city that had taught her so much about light and darkness. The storm had passed, leaving a renewed sense of clarity that she hoped would permeate Barcelona's storied walls. Her journey through the shadows had revealed the light, and in that light, she found her true calling.

# Chapter 21: New Horizons

In the weeks following her transformative exhibit, Mia's studio saw a ceaseless flow of visitors—artists, students, journalists, and art lovers, all eager to engage with the woman who had bravely uncovered one of the biggest art scandals in recent history. Each interaction reinforced Mia's newfound role as a mentor and advocate for ethical art practices, a role she embraced with humility and a deep sense of responsibility.

Amidst this flurry of activity, an intriguing opportunity presented itself. Mia received an invitation from the Barcelona City Council to spearhead a new initiative aimed at promoting transparency and education in the art market. It was an honor and a challenge that promised to extend her influence far beyond her studio and even the city itself.

Mia mulled over the offer in her now-quiet studio, the evening light casting long shadows across the floor. This was a chance to enact lasting change, to help prevent others from falling into the same traps that had ensnared Lucia and so many others. Yet, it also meant stepping further into a public role that demanded much of her time and energy, which could distance her from the very essence of her own artistry.

As she pondered, Javier dropped by, bringing with him a sense of comfort and familiarity. "It's a big decision," he acknowledged, looking over the letter from the council. "But think of the good you could do, Mia."

Mia nodded, her fingers tracing the edge of her canvas. "I know, and I want to help. I just worry about losing my way, forgetting why I started painting in the first place."

Javier smiled, his eyes warm and understanding. "You once told me that your art is about expressing truths, revealing the unseen. Isn't this just another canvas for you? A bigger one, perhaps, where you can draw broader strokes for a greater good?"

His words struck a chord in Mia, giving her the perspective she needed. It wasn't about choosing between her art and her advocacy; it was about merging them, using each to fuel and inform the other.

With her decision made, Mia accepted the council's offer. The following weeks were a whirlwind of meetings and planning sessions. Mia worked closely with art historians, educators, and legal experts to develop a comprehensive program that included artist workshops, public lectures, and a new verification system for galleries and auctions.

The initiative was met with enthusiasm and a few skeptics, but Mia's genuine passion and proven commitment gradually won most of her critics over. The project not only aimed to educate but also to rebuild trust in a market that had been shadowed by doubt.

As the new program launched, Mia took a moment during the opening ceremony to reflect on the journey that had brought her here. The gallery was filled with vibrant discussions and the air buzzed with ideas for the future—a stark contrast to the somber revelations of past months.

Later, as the guests departed, Mia returned to her studio. The walls were adorned with her latest works, each piece a testament to her growth not only as an artist but as a person who had dared to confront the darkness within her world. Alone, she picked up her brushes and began to paint. The canvas before her was blank, a new beginning waiting to be shaped.

With each stroke, Mia realized that her role was not just to reform the art world but to inspire others to take their own stand, to fight for authenticity and truth in whatever form it might take. Her art, once a solitary pursuit, had become a beacon, guiding not just her own way, but lighting paths for others to follow.

As the night deepened, Mia stepped back from her new painting. It was vibrant, bold, and unapologetically truthful. Just like her.

# Chapter 22: The Canvas of Tomorrow

As the new initiative gained momentum, Mia found herself at the intersection of art and activism, her days filled with engagements that ranged from inspiring young artists in workshops to discussing policy with cultural leaders. The transformative power of her role brought a fresh sense of purpose, but it also left her little time for the solitary work that had defined her as a painter.

One crisp morning, as Mia prepared for a seminar on art authenticity, she received a call from an old friend, Clara, a fellow artist who had watched Mia's journey with both admiration and concern. "Mia, it's been too long," Clara's voice crackled over the line, a warm reminder of less complicated times. "I've been watching all the incredible things you're doing. How about a break? Let's visit the old studio route this weekend, just like old times."

The invitation was a lifeline thrown in the midst of her whirlwind schedule. Mia accepted eagerly, craving the simplicity and camaraderie that had first sparked her love for art.

That weekend, as they wandered through familiar haunts and discovered new studios together, Clara and Mia discussed everything from the latest techniques to the ongoing challenges in the art community. It was during one such conversation, in a small, sunlit studio overlooking the Mediterranean, that Mia had a revelation.

"Sometimes I miss just being in my studio, lost in my work, not worrying about forgeries or scandals," Mia confessed, watching the sunlight play over the ocean.

Clara nodded, understanding her friend's conflict. "But you're doing so much good, Mia. And maybe there's a way to blend these parts of your life more seamlessly."

Mia turned to her friend, curious. "What do you mean?"

"Use your art to talk about these issues directly. Create a series that explores the themes of authenticity, trust, and integrity. Your art has always been powerful, Mia. It can speak these truths profoundly," Clara suggested, her eyes alight with creative fervor.

The idea resonated with Mia, the concept melding her dual roles into a cohesive vision. Inspired, she returned to her studio with a new project in mind. This series would be more than just paintings; it would be a narrative, each piece telling a story of the art world's shadows and lights.

Over the following weeks, Mia threw herself into her new series. She explored the complex interplay of colors and forms to depict the tension between reality and illusion, the genuine and the counterfeit. Each canvas became a dialogue, inviting viewers to look deeper and question what lay beneath the surface.

As the series neared completion, Mia planned an exhibit unlike any other she had hosted before. It would not only showcase her new works but also include panels and discussions on the importance of authenticity in art. She reached out to experts, activists, and fellow artists to contribute, turning the exhibit into a cultural event that drew attention from far beyond Barcelona.

The opening night of the exhibit was a culmination of all Mia had learned and fought for. The gallery was packed with an eager audience, their eyes moving thoughtfully from piece to piece, engaging in animated discussions about the implications of each work.

Mia walked among her guests, her heart full as she observed the impact of her art. The conversations around her were proof that her paintings did more than fill space on a wall—they sparked thought, dialogue, and perhaps even change.

Standing beside her latest creation, a vibrant depiction of a phoenix rising from ashes, Mia felt a profound connection to her work. This painting symbolized her own rebirth, her evolution from a solitary artist to a pivotal figure in the fight for artistic integrity.

The night wound down with heartfelt applause and many congratulations, but for Mia, the true success was not in the praise but in the knowledge that her art was making a difference. She had found a way to weave her passion for painting with her commitment to advocacy, each enhancing the other, creating a tapestry rich with meaning and purpose.

As the last guests departed and the gallery lights dimmed, Mia stood alone, surrounded by her creations. Her journey had taught her that being an artist was not just about mastering the brush, but about embracing the power of art to reveal, challenge, and transform. Tomorrow, she would return to her canvas, ready to explore new horizons, forever changed, forever driven by the quest for truth in art and in life.

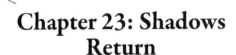

# Chapter 23: Shadows Return

As autumn embraced Barcelona with its cooler breezes and shorter days, Mia found herself once again caught between the dual worlds of creation and investigation. The success of her exhibit had not only solidified her position as an influential figure in the art community but had also inadvertently drawn her deeper into the complexities of art fraud, an arena fraught with more dangers than she had anticipated.

One late October evening, while Mia was alone in her studio, meticulously sketching out her next project, an unexpected visitor appeared at her door. It was Inspector Llorente, and the grave expression on his face immediately told Mia that this was no casual visit.

"Mia, I'm sorry to intrude, but we've had a development that I think you should be aware of," Llorente began, his hat in his hands, a sign of the seriousness of the situation. "There's been another incident. A prominent collector found one of the pieces they purchased at a charity auction last year is a forgery. And it's not just any forgery; the style points directly to the ring we thought we had dismantled."

Mia felt a cold shiver run down her spine. The news was a stark reminder that the roots of corruption might be deeper and more entangled than they had feared. "Do we know how many more forgeries are out there?" she asked, her mind racing with the implications.

"We don't, not yet," Llorente admitted. "But this isn't an isolated incident. Two other pieces have been identified as forgeries in the past week. We're looking at a potential resurgence of the forgery ring, or perhaps a fragment that continued operating in the shadows."

The resurgence of the forgery ring meant not only a failure in eradicating the corruption but also a direct threat to the progress Mia and her colleagues had strived to achieve in rebuilding trust within the art community. The thought weighed heavily on her, a gnawing worry that her efforts might unravel.

"Is there anything specific you need from me?" Mia asked, already knowing that her involvement was inevitable.

"Yes," Llorente replied, his gaze steady and serious. "I need you to help us verify the authenticity of several pieces that were sold at auctions and exhibits over the last year. Your expertise has been invaluable, and we could use your eye to spot any more fakes that might still be circulating."

Mia nodded, her sense of duty overriding her initial shock. "Of course, I'll help in any way I can."

As Llorente outlined their immediate plan, Mia felt the familiar pull of the detective role she had come to accept. The next few days were a blur of activity. Mia visited galleries, auction houses, and private collections, her trained eye scanning for discrepancies and tell-tale signs of forgery. Each discovery of a counterfeit piece felt like a personal affront, a reminder of the ongoing battle against deceit in the art world.

During her investigations, Mia encountered whispers of a mysterious figure known only as "The Artisan," purportedly the mastermind behind the new wave of forgeries. This elusive character seemed always one step ahead, and Mia's frustration grew with each dead end.

One evening, over coffee in a dimly lit café, Mia met with Llorente to discuss their progress, or lack thereof. "It's like chasing a ghost," Mia confessed, her fatigue evident in her voice. "Every lead we follow, The Artisan slips away. It's as if they know our every move."

Llorente shared her frustration. "It's a clever adversary, Mia. But every criminal makes a mistake eventually. We just need to be patient and vigilant."

Mia sipped her coffee, her gaze lost in the steam rising from the cup. The challenge was daunting, but her resolve was firm. "We'll catch this Artisan," she said quietly, more to herself than to Llorente. "We have to."

As the night deepened and the café began to empty, Mia and Llorente planned their next steps, unaware that eyes watched them from the shadows, calculating and cold. The game of cat and mouse was well underway, and Mia was determined to lead the charge, her artistic soul fused with a detective's determination to unearth the truth hidden beneath layers of deceit and paint.

# Chapter 24: The Artisan's Trail

As autumn gave way to the chillier embraces of winter, Mia found herself more entrenched than ever in the unraveling mystery of the forgery ring's resurgence. The clues pointing to "The Artisan" were scattered, cryptic, leading Mia and Inspector Llorente through a maze of dead ends and false starts that tested their resolve.

During one late-night session at the police station, Mia pored over files and auction records, searching for any pattern that might reveal the Artisan's method or motivation. Each document seemed to whisper secrets just beyond grasp, like shadows flitting at the edge of vision. "There has to be something we're missing," Mia muttered, her eyes weary from hours of scrutiny.

Inspector Llorente, equally frustrated but always patient, joined her at the table, spreading out a city map dotted with locations of discovered forgeries. "We've been assuming the Artisan is working alone, but what if that's not the case? What if there's a network supporting them?"

Mia considered this, her mind racing through the implications. "A network would mean a deeper level of organization, possibly even insiders at auctions and galleries. We could be looking at a syndicate, not just a lone forger."

Motivated by this new angle, they began re-examining the evidence with a broader scope, considering connections they had previously overlooked. As they delved deeper into the auction house employees' backgrounds and their associations, one name began to recur with suspicious frequency: Marco Silvetti, a respected art handler known for his expertise in restoration.

"Silvetti has had access to every major auction where a forgery was later identified," Llorente noted, circling the name on a list. "And he's skilled enough in restoration techniques to alter artworks without leaving obvious traces."

The next step was clear. Mia and Llorente decided to bring Silvetti in for questioning, hoping he might shed light on the Artisan's operations or even confirm his involvement. The interview, however, proved to be more challenging than anticipated. Silvetti was smooth, his answers rehearsed and too polished, a performance perfected by years in an industry that valued appearance over authenticity.

Despite his slick responses, Mia noticed a flicker of unease when they mentioned the Artisan. "We know about your connections, Marco. It's only a matter of time before we find enough to link you directly to the forgeries," she pressed, watching his reaction closely.

Silvetti's façade cracked, just for a moment, and his glance darted to a file on the table—a file that contained a partial fingerprint found on the back of a forged painting. It was the slip Mia had been waiting for. "You seem particularly interested in that file," she observed pointedly.

Under the weight of their scrutiny, Silvetti's composure began to crumble. "I don't know anything about an Artisan," he finally blurted, his voice a mixture of defiance and fear. "I was just asked to make a few adjustments, that's all. Artistic enhancements, not forgeries."

"By whom?" Llorente pressed, seizing the opening.

Silvetti hesitated, then sighed, the fight draining from him. "A collector. He promised it would be harmless. I never knew the paintings would be sold as originals."

This confession blew the case wide open, leading Mia and Llorente into the murky waters of high-stakes collectors and duplicitous deals that transcended national borders. The puzzle was complex, but with each piece that fell into place, they drew closer to the Artisan.

As winter deepened and the first snows began to fall, Mia walked through the quiet streets of Barcelona, her breath forming small clouds in the cold air. The city with its hidden depths and deceptive appearances was a reminder of the art it housed—beautiful, multifaceted, and sometimes, painted with lies. But like any skilled artist, Mia knew that persistence could reveal the truth beneath the surface, no matter how well it was hidden. With each step, she was ready to face whatever challenges lay ahead, her resolve as unyielding as the winter chill.

# Chapter 25: A Cold Trail Warms

The revelation from Marco Silvetti had added crucial momentum to Mia's investigation. With the knowledge that a collector was involved, the scope of the inquiry broadened significantly, suggesting that the forgeries were not just the work of a rogue artist but part of a larger, more orchestrated criminal enterprise.

With winter tightening its grip on Barcelona, the city's festive decorations contrasted sharply with the grim task at hand. Mia and Inspector Llorente, now armed with new leads, focused on tracing the collector Silvetti had mentioned. The trail led them to Antoni Gaudell, a prominent figure in the Barcelona art scene known for his extensive private collection and philanthropic endeavors.

Mia felt a pang of disbelief. Gaudell was a respected benefactor of the arts, his name synonymous with generosity and integrity. The idea that he could be involved in such a scandal was difficult to digest, yet the evidence was increasingly compelling.

Llorente arranged surveillance on Gaudell and initiated a discreet inquiry into his financial affairs and recent acquisitions. Meanwhile, Mia continued her work in the art community, her role as a liaison becoming ever more vital as she navigated the delicate networks of trust and reputation.

During a charity gala, an event Gaudell hosted annually, Mia had the opportunity to observe him up close. The lavish affair, filled with the elite of Barcelona's society, was a testament to Gaudell's influence.

Mia mingled among the guests, her artist's eye now attuned to the subtleties of deception.

Gaudell was the perfect host, charming and attentive. However, Mia noticed a certain tension in his interactions when the conversation veered close to art authenticity. It was a fleeting look, a momentary lapse that most would miss, but to Mia, it was a telltale sign.

After the event, Mia shared her observations with Llorente. "He's careful, very controlled. But there's something off. I could sense it," she explained.

"Good instincts," Llorente responded, nodding. "We've found irregularities in his financials—payments that coincide with auction dates where forgeries later appeared. We're close, Mia. We just need more concrete evidence."

The break they needed came unexpectedly. A junior officer reviewing security footage from another unrelated case spotted Gaudell in a compromising position—meeting with an unknown individual in a secluded part of town, exchanging what appeared to be documents. The footage wasn't conclusive enough for an arrest, but it provided the leverage they needed.

Llorente and Mia confronted Gaudell with the footage. Faced with the growing evidence against him, Gaudell's composure finally cracked. He confessed to being part of a network that commissioned forgeries to launder money through the art market. The Artisan, he revealed, was not one person but a pseudonym used by various artists employed by the network to create forgeries.

"This goes deeper than we thought," Llorente said grimly as they processed Gaudell's statement at the station. "It's not just about forgeries. It's about money laundering, corruption... This is going to shake the art world globally."

Mia felt a mix of relief and dread. The mystery of the Artisan was solved, but the implications were overwhelming. The art world she loved was about to undergo a seismic shift, and she was at its epicenter.

As she left the police station, the city around her felt different. The lights of the holiday season shone brightly, casting shadows that seemed to dance mockingly on the snow-dusted streets. Mia walked home, her mind heavy with the knowledge that her work was far from over. The forgeries were just the beginning, and the true challenge lay in restoring integrity to an art world riddled with shadows. She was ready to face that challenge, armed with her unwavering commitment to truth and the beauty of genuine art.

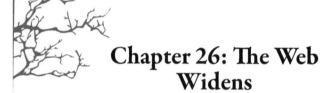

# Chapter 26: The Web Widens

As the revelations about the extensive forgery network and its ties to money laundering began to unravel, the art community worldwide braced itself for the impact. Mia, once isolated in her pursuit of authenticity in art, now found herself at the forefront of a global dialogue about the integrity of the art market. Her role had evolved from a local artist to an international advocate for transparency and ethics in art.

Inspector Llorente and Mia continued their collaboration, driven by the urgent need to dismantle the network that Antoni Gaudell had exposed. Their focus shifted towards identifying other members and tracing the laundered money, a task that spanned continents and involved cooperation with international law enforcement agencies.

One chilly morning, Mia met with Llorente at a quiet café, a far cry from the police stations and formal meetings that had dominated their interactions. The informal setting was a brief respite from the intensity of their work. "We've made significant progress," Llorente began, his eyes reflecting both fatigue and determination. "Interpol is involved now, and several arrests have been made in Europe and beyond. The network is larger than we anticipated, but we're making headway."

Mia sipped her coffee, the steam warming her face. "It's overwhelming," she admitted. "When I started this, I never imagined it would lead here."

"It's a testament to your courage and commitment," Llorente replied sincerely. "You've changed the landscape of art protection forever."

Their conversation was interrupted by a call. Llorente listened intently, his expression turning grave. After a brief exchange, he hung up and turned to Mia. "They found another stash of forgeries, this time in a warehouse in Berlin. They're linked to several known pieces in your investigations."

The news was disheartening but not surprising. Mia had learned to brace herself for the continuous unfolding of the network's reach. "What's our next step?" she asked, ready to continue the fight.

"We consolidate all the evidence for the prosecutions, and we keep tracking the money. It's the key to uncovering more members of the network," Llorente explained.

As the winter progressed, Mia's studio became a hub not only for her art but also for strategy sessions with law enforcement and art security experts. Despite the gravity of her role, Mia made sure to carve out time for her painting, which remained her sanctuary and source of strength.

During one such painting session, Mia reflected on the journey that had brought her here. Each brushstroke on her canvas was a reminder of the path she had traveled—from uncovering the initial forgery to exposing a global scandal. Art had always been her way of communicating with the world, and now it served as a record of her fight for justice.

The exhibition of her latest series was approaching, and Mia planned it as a narrative of her journey through the realms of art and crime. The showcase would feature her paintings alongside artifacts and documents from the case, each piece telling a story of challenge and triumph.

On the eve of the exhibition, Mia walked through the gallery, arranging the final pieces. The walls told a story of resilience, each canvas a testament to the power of persistence and truth. As she adjusted the lighting on a painting depicting a fragmented vase being pieced back together—a metaphor for the art world's current state of repair—she felt a profound connection to her work.

The exhibition opened to critical acclaim, drawing attention from around the world. Visitors from various countries walked the halls, each pausing to absorb the powerful messages behind Mia's art. Critics wrote about the unique blend of visual art and investigative narrative, calling it a groundbreaking approach to discussing global issues through art.

As Mia mingled with the guests, answering questions and discussing her inspirations, she realized how far-reaching her impact had been. She had started as an artist in her small studio in Barcelona, but her journey had led her to become a pivotal figure in a crucial global issue.

The fight against art forgery and corruption was far from over, but Mia knew she had ignited a spark that would continue to grow, fueled by the collective efforts of those who valued truth and integrity in art. Her canvas was no longer just a piece of fabric stretched over a frame; it was a living, evolving testament to the resilience and enduring power of authenticity.

# Chapter 27: Undercover Canvas

Following the success of her groundbreaking exhibition, Mia found herself increasingly viewed not just as an artist, but as a crusader for authenticity in the art world. Her unique blend of artistic talent and investigative prowess had not only illuminated the dark corners of art forgery but had also inspired others to take a stand. However, the deeper she ventured into this shadowy realm, the more complex and perilous her journey became.

The latest development came unexpectedly one evening while Mia was in her studio, lost in thought over a canvas that captured the tumultuous waves of her recent experiences. Her phone rang, cutting through the silence with its insistent tone. It was Inspector Llorente, and his voice carried an urgency that immediately set Mia on edge.

"Mia, we need your help with something delicate," Llorente began, his words measured. "There's an upcoming auction in Paris. We suspect it will be a prime target for the forgery ring to try and unload some high-value pieces."

Mia listened intently, her brush pausing mid-stroke. "What do you need me to do?"

"We believe an insider might be involved, someone with access to the auction house's operations. We need someone who can blend in, observe, and perhaps uncover who this insider might be. Given your reputation and expertise, you're uniquely suited for this role," Llorente explained.

The proposition was daunting. Going undercover meant stepping directly into the lion's den, where a single misstep could not only jeopardize the mission but also put her in grave danger. Yet, Mia knew that if there was a chance to help dismantle the network further, she had to take it.

"I'll do it," she said finally, her decision firm. "When do we start?"

Preparations began swiftly. Mia was briefed on every known associate of the forgery ring, familiarizing herself with their backgrounds, their methods, and most importantly, their interests in art. She also underwent training on the finer points of undercover work, learning how to communicate subtly with law enforcement while maintaining her cover.

The auction in Paris was one of the grandest events of the season, attracting collectors, dealers, and art enthusiasts from around the world. Mia arrived dressed elegantly, her role as a prominent artist her best disguise. As she mingled with the guests, her eyes and ears were open for any sign of illicit activity or familiar faces from Llorente's briefings.

Throughout the evening, Mia engaged in discussions about art trends and upcoming artists, all the while watching for the behaviors Llorente had described. It was during a conversation about the resurgence of classical techniques in modern art that she noticed a man whose demeanor seemed oddly out of place.

He was too interested in the logistics of the auction—specifically the security measures and the transport arrangements for purchased pieces. Mia casually steered the conversation towards more general topics, all while noting his features and his reactions.

After the man excused himself, Mia slipped away to send a quick message to Llorente, describing the man and his inquiries. It wasn't long before she received a confirmation; he was indeed one of the persons of interest.

The auction proceeded without a hitch, and Mia continued her role flawlessly. It was only after the final gavel had fallen and the guests began to depart that Llorente and his team moved in, detaining the suspicious individual and several others based on the intelligence Mia had gathered.

Back in Barcelona, as Mia reflected on the operation, she felt a mix of relief and exhaustion. Her painting that evening was more introspective, a complex interplay of shadows and light, mirroring the dual nature of her life now intertwined with art and espionage.

The successful intervention in Paris was a significant victory, but the battle against art forgery was far from over. Mia knew that each operation, each brushstroke on canvas, was a step towards restoring integrity to the art world. Her life had taken on a broader scope, her art a deeper meaning, as she continued to navigate the delicate balance between beauty and truth.

# Chapter 28: Layers Unveiled

In the weeks following the Paris operation, the art world buzzed with whispers of the dramatic intervention that had prevented a significant forgery from entering the market. Mia's role, though kept confidential to protect her safety and future operations, had elevated her status among the few privy to the details. However, with recognition came increased responsibility and scrutiny, something Mia felt deeply as she continued her work both as an artist and an unofficial consultant to law enforcement.

Back in her Barcelona studio, which had become a sanctuary and a command center, Mia was meticulously planning her next series of works, inspired by her undercover experiences. Each canvas was designed to capture the essence of her dual life—subtle hints of darkness and light, revealing the complexities of her journey into the underworld of art forgery.

One crisp morning, Mia received an unexpected visitor at her studio. It was Detective Elena Márquez, a member of Llorente's team, known for her sharp intellect and dedication. Elena's presence usually meant new developments, and today was no exception.

"Mia, we've been analyzing the network's activities based on the information you helped uncover in Paris," Elena began, her tone serious as she laid out a series of documents on Mia's worktable. "We've traced a series of transactions that lead to an art foundation in Switzerland. It appears to be a front for laundering money through art sales."

The revelation was a significant piece of the puzzle, suggesting that the network was more extensive and complex than previously thought. Mia reviewed the documents, her mind racing with the implications. "Do you think this foundation could be the key to dismantling the network?"

"It's possible," Elena replied. "But we need more concrete evidence before we can take action. We believe there might be a ledger or some record of the transactions. If we could get our hands on that, it would be a game-changer."

Mia nodded, understanding the challenge they faced. "What's the plan?"

"We're arranging an operation to investigate the foundation discreetly. Given your expertise and recent experience, we'd like you to be part of the team. You would be invaluable in helping us identify any suspicious artworks or documents," Elena explained, her gaze steady.

Mia felt a mix of apprehension and resolve. Going into another operation meant facing potential danger, but the opportunity to strike at the heart of the forgery network was too important to pass up. "I'll do it," she affirmed, her voice steady.

The following weeks were a blur of preparation and strategy. Mia, Elena, and the rest of the team worked closely, planning each detail of the operation. Finally, they traveled to Switzerland, the picturesque landscapes a stark contrast to the seriousness of their mission.

The operation took place under the guise of a routine audit by a fictitious regulatory body. Mia and Elena, posing as auditors, were granted access to the foundation's archives. As they examined the artworks and scrutinized financial records, Mia's trained eye caught a series of anomalies in the provenance documents of several high-value pieces.

Working swiftly, they gathered enough evidence to confirm their suspicions—forged documents, altered ownership records, and encrypted files that hinted at the broader network's reach. With meticulous care, they documented everything, ensuring that nothing was overlooked.

As they wrapped up their investigation, Mia felt a profound sense of accomplishment mixed with relief. The operation had been risky, but successful. They had secured the evidence needed to expose not just the foundation but potentially the entire network.

Upon returning to Barcelona, Mia resumed her work in her studio, each stroke of her brush infused with the experiences she had lived through. The upcoming exhibition of her new series promised to be her most personal yet, reflecting the depths of her journey into the shadows of the art world.

As Mia painted, she knew that her actions had helped protect the integrity of the art she loved so much. The road ahead remained uncertain, fraught with challenges and dangers, but Mia was ready. Her art, her courage, and her commitment to truth were her guides, lighting her path forward as she continued to fight against the darkness, one brushstroke at a time.

# Chapter 29: The Geneva Reveal

The successful operation in Switzerland had a ripple effect throughout the international art community, shedding light on a hidden world of forgery and corruption that stretched across continents. With solid evidence in hand and an extensive network beginning to unravel, Mia felt a profound mix of triumph and trepidation as she prepared for the fallout.

Back in Barcelona, the impact of her recent undercover work was becoming evident. The local art scene, once vibrant and bustling, now carried an air of caution and reflection. Galleries tightened their acquisition protocols, and collectors became more scrupulous about the provenance of artworks. Mia's studio, meanwhile, turned into a place of pilgrimage for many who sought to understand the complexities of art authenticity.

Amid this transformative period, Mia received an invitation to speak at an international conference on art and legality held in Geneva, close to the epicenter of her recent operation. It was an opportunity to share her insights and experiences with a broader audience, and Mia accepted, seeing it as a chance to further her advocacy for transparency in the art market.

Arriving in Geneva, Mia was greeted by the crisp air and pristine streets, a stark contrast to the murky dealings she had uncovered just weeks before. The conference venue, a grand hall adorned with artworks that celebrated European heritage, was filled with art professionals, legal experts, and law enforcement officials from around the world.

When it was her turn to speak, Mia stepped up to the podium with a quiet confidence. She began by recounting her journey as an artist inadvertently drawn into the shadowy side of the art world. She detailed her collaborative efforts with the police, the challenges of going undercover, and the personal risks involved in exposing a global forgery ring.

"The world of art is bound by an intrinsic value that transcends monetary worth," Mia stated, her voice resonating in the packed hall. "When that trust is violated through forgery, it's not just the buyers who are defrauded—it's every artist, every viewer, and every participant in the cultural dialogue."

Her speech was met with rapt attention and, ultimately, a standing ovation. The audience was moved by her passion and commitment to safeguarding the art world. After her presentation, Mia participated in panel discussions, offering her perspective on improving international cooperation in art crime investigations.

During one of the breaks, Mia was approached by a Swiss investigator, André Baumgartner, who had been instrumental in the groundwork for the Swiss operation. "Your work has opened doors we didn't even know were there," André remarked, his expression earnest. "We've started to implement new checks and balances in our art markets because of your findings."

Mia smiled, grateful for the recognition but aware of the long road ahead. "It's a start, André. But there's much more to do. We need to keep pushing for transparency and accountability."

The conference concluded with a call to action, urging international bodies to adopt stricter regulations and enforcement mechanisms to combat art forgery. Mia left Geneva feeling energized and hopeful, knowing that her efforts had sparked a global conversation.

Returning to Barcelona, Mia was welcomed back to her studio with a newfound reverence. She resumed her painting, each brushstroke imbued with a sense of purpose. Her next series of artworks, inspired by her experiences in Geneva, aimed to capture the essence of change and resilience in the face of adversity.

As Mia painted, she reflected on the journey that had brought her here. From the quiet confines of her studio to the global stage, she had not only exposed a criminal network but had also evolved as an artist and advocate. Her life had become an intricate tapestry of art and activism, each influencing and enriching the other. And as she prepared for her upcoming exhibition, Mia knew that her story was still unfolding, with each new chapter promising further challenges and triumphs in her ongoing quest for truth in art.

# Chapter 30: The Fabric of Trust

After the conference in Geneva, the art world's focus on forgery and transparency intensified. Mia's role in this transformation had solidified her as a pivotal figure in advocating for systemic changes within the industry. Her return to Barcelona was marked not only by a deeper commitment to her art but also by invitations to collaborate with various international bodies dedicated to safeguarding cultural heritage.

Back in her studio, surrounded by the familiar smells of paint and turpentine, Mia began working on a new series that reflected her journey and the lessons learned along the way. This series, titled "The Fabric of Trust," aimed to explore the delicate interplay between authenticity and deception, a theme that resonated deeply with her recent experiences.

As Mia delved into her work, she received a call from Inspector Llorente, who had been following up on the leads exposed by the Swiss operation. "Mia, we've made significant progress," he announced. "Thanks to the information gathered during the Geneva conference, we've been able to identify additional members of the forgery network spread across Europe."

Mia listened intently, a mix of satisfaction and concern in her voice. "That's great news, Carlos. How can I assist further?"

"We could use your expertise to verify a batch of artworks recovered in raids across Italy and Germany," Llorente explained. "Your eye for detail could help us determine which pieces are authentic and which are forgeries."

Eager to contribute, Mia agreed to assist, and arrangements were made for her to visit the police's secure art storage facility. There, amidst rows of confiscated artworks, Mia meticulously examined each piece, applying her knowledge to discern subtle inconsistencies and alterations. Her work proved invaluable, helping to classify numerous artworks and providing crucial evidence for the ongoing investigations.

The impact of Mia's findings was significant, leading to further arrests and the recovery of stolen artworks. Her ability to bridge the gap between art and law enforcement had become a cornerstone of the fight against art crime.

Emboldened by these successes, Mia organized a symposium in Barcelona, bringing together artists, gallery owners, curators, and law enforcement officials. The event focused on fostering a collaborative approach to preventing art forgery, emphasizing the importance of education and rigorous provenance research.

The symposium was a resounding success, sparking lively discussions and commitments from various stakeholders to adopt more stringent verification processes. Mia's keynote speech, in which she shared her personal and professional insights, underscored the collective responsibility of the art community to uphold integrity and trust.

As winter gave way to spring, Mia's new series "The Fabric of Trust" was unveiled at a major exhibition. The collection was met with critical acclaim, celebrated not only for its artistic merit but also for its poignant commentary on the art world's vulnerabilities and strengths. Visitors were particularly drawn to a piece titled "Veil of Veracity," a striking composition that used layers of translucent materials to represent the uncovering of truth.

Amidst the success, Mia remained grounded, her thoughts often returning to the ongoing challenges faced by the art community. She knew that the fight against forgery was far from over, but she also recognized the progress that had been made, much of it sparked by her courage and determination.

One evening, as she stood alone in her studio, reflecting on the path she had traveled, Mia felt a deep connection to her role as an artist and advocate. The journey had been arduous and fraught with danger, but it had also been immensely rewarding. She realized that her impact extended beyond the canvas; it wove through the very fabric of the art community, strengthening the bonds of trust and integrity that held it together.

With a contented sigh, Mia cleaned her brushes and prepared for the next day, ready to continue her work with renewed vigor. The journey was ongoing, and Mia was committed to playing her part in shaping a more transparent, honest, and vibrant art world.

# Chapter 31: The Network Unravels

In the wake of the symposium and the success of her exhibition, Mia's influence continued to grow. Not only was she now recognized as a pivotal figure in the fight against art forgery, but her art had also become a symbol of integrity and resilience. The threads of her story were weaving a broader tapestry of awareness and action across the global art community.

One sunny afternoon, while Mia was deep in thought over a new canvas, her concentration was interrupted by a knock at her studio door. Opening it, she found Inspector Llorente, accompanied by a young woman whose earnest expression was framed by a keen attentiveness.

"Mia, good afternoon," Llorente greeted her, his usual seriousness softened by a smile. "I'd like you to meet Sophie Renaud, an investigator from Interpol. She's been leading some of the international efforts tied to our case."

Sophie extended her hand, her grip firm and confident. "It's an honor to meet you, Ms. Valdés. Your work has been instrumental in our broader investigations."

Mia welcomed them in, curious about the visit. "How can I help you today?"

"We have some good news," Sophie began as they settled around Mia's worktable, strewn with sketches and paint tubes. "Thanks to the leads generated from your efforts and the symposium discussions, we've made substantial progress. We've dismantled a major part of the network responsible for the forgery ring that affected so many."

Llorente nodded in agreement. "We've managed to trace the financial transactions back to a few key players who were using the art market to launder money. Several arrests have been made across Europe, and numerous artworks have been recovered."

Mia absorbed the news with a mixture of relief and satisfaction. "That's wonderful to hear. The damage these networks have done to the art community is profound."

"There's more," Sophie added, pulling a folder from her bag. "We've also uncovered evidence that suggests this network may have been involved in other criminal activities, including the illegal trade of cultural artifacts. We believe they've been using similar methods to move these items across borders."

This new angle introduced a layer of complexity to the already intricate situation. Mia felt a renewed sense of duty stir within her. "Is there anything specific you need from me at this point?"

"Actually, yes," Sophie responded, opening the folder to reveal photographs of various artifacts. "We could use your help in identifying some of these items. Your expertise could help us determine their origin and perhaps their last legitimate whereabouts."

Mia agreed without hesitation, driven by her commitment to restoring integrity to all aspects of the art and cultural heritage world. Over the next few hours, they worked together, Mia providing insights and suggestions based on her knowledge and experience.

As the session came to an end, Llorente and Sophie prepared to leave, their expressions a mix of fatigue and determination. "We'll keep you updated on our progress," Llorente promised. "And again, thank you, Mia. Your involvement has changed the course of this investigation."

After they left, Mia returned to her canvas, her mind alive with the complexities of the day's revelations. The landscape of her painting seemed to echo the unfolding landscape of her life—vivid, layered, and endlessly evolving.

In the days that followed, Mia continued her collaboration with international agencies, her studio becoming a crossroads of art, law enforcement, and cultural preservation. The impact of her work reached beyond the canvases she painted, helping to mend the very fabric of an international community shaken by deceit.

Her efforts were not just about cleaning up the art world; they were about restoring faith in the cultural expressions that connect humanity across time and space. As she painted, Mia realized that each stroke was a testament to the power of resilience and truth, a power that could indeed bring light to the darkest of corners.

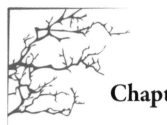

# Chapter 32: Hidden Threads

The gravity of what Mia had learned about the forgery ring's connection to illicit antiquities trading weighed heavily on her mind in the days that followed. She recognized the enormity of the issue, its implications rippling far beyond the confines of the art world. The artifacts tied to this network carried with them the cultural heritage of entire regions, and their loss was a blow to history itself.

Amid this sobering realization, Mia maintained her artistic pursuits, channeling the complexities of her thoughts into her canvases. She knew that her art could convey messages that words alone could not, and each painting became a narrative of defiance against those who sought to exploit culture for profit.

While she worked, Inspector Llorente and Sophie Renaud remained in close contact, updating Mia on the ongoing investigation. Their collaborative efforts had borne fruit; new leads were emerging as more members of the network were identified and apprehended.

One morning, Sophie arrived at Mia's studio with a sense of urgency in her step. "Mia, we need your help again," she said, her expression serious. "We've uncovered another series of financial transactions connected to a group posing as an art restoration firm. They appear to be exporting artifacts to private buyers."

Mia listened attentively as Sophie laid out the evidence, a mix of documents and photographs that painted a troubling picture. "They claim to offer restoration services to collectors, but in reality, they're smuggling artifacts. These transactions lead back to a private collection in London."

Mia studied the images, recognizing some of the artifacts as pieces she had seen in academic journals. "This is devastating," she said softly. "Each one of these items represents a piece of history stolen from its rightful place."

Sophie nodded grimly. "We need to uncover their network and prevent more artifacts from disappearing. Your expertise could help us identify which items might be targeted next."

Mia agreed to assist, and over the next few days, she worked with Sophie and Llorente to cross-reference records, research auction catalogs, and build a timeline of suspect transactions. The effort was painstaking but revealed a disturbing pattern: the smuggling operation was far more systematic than they had initially thought, reaching into reputable galleries and private collections.

Finally, they decided to confront the London-based collector suspected of being the key buyer. Mia's presence was crucial, as her expertise lent credibility to the law enforcement team. The collector, a man named Edward Livingston, had cultivated a reputation as an eccentric but ethical enthusiast.

During the confrontation, Mia and Llorente presented their evidence to Livingston, whose initial shock quickly turned to indignation. "This is absurd!" he protested. "I've acquired every piece legally and through trusted intermediaries!"

"That may be what you believe, but the documentation we have paints a different story," Llorente countered, unfazed.

Mia stepped forward, her voice calm but firm. "Mr. Livingston, some of these artifacts have provenance issues that can't be ignored. I know you care about art and history, and I believe you've been misled. Please, work with us to uncover the truth."

Livingston hesitated, the conflict clear on his face. Finally, he relented, agreeing to cooperate in exchange for leniency.

With Livingston's assistance, they were able to identify the key figures orchestrating the smuggling operation and recover several artifacts before they could be shipped abroad. The success of this intervention strengthened Mia's resolve and reinforced her commitment to cultural preservation.

Returning to Barcelona, Mia felt a renewed sense of purpose as she stood before her easel. Her latest series of paintings took on new layers of meaning, each canvas revealing the hidden threads of history, the unseen connections that bind past and present. She understood now that her role was not just to expose deceit but also to weave together the stories of art and culture that connect humanity across time.

Mia painted late into the night, the strokes on her canvas telling a story of resilience, integrity, and the enduring power of truth.

# Chapter 33: The Unraveling

The triumph of exposing the smuggling ring in London filled Mia with hope, but she remained cautious. Every victory brought her closer to understanding the scale of the network, yet each layer unveiled also revealed how much deeper the corruption ran. She continued her collaboration with Inspector Llorente and Sophie Renaud, the trio forming a resilient partnership determined to see justice served.

One afternoon, as Mia was putting the finishing touches on her latest painting—a vivid depiction of an ancient artifact emerging from shadows—she received a call from Llorente. "Mia, we need to meet. There's been another development," he said, his voice hinting at urgency.

Mia quickly arranged to meet with Llorente and Sophie at a small café near her studio. Upon arrival, she found them waiting, their expressions solemn.

"We've traced another series of transactions leading to a new player in the forgery network," Sophie began, sliding a dossier across the table. "It's someone we hadn't suspected, but they seem to be crucial in coordinating the movement of art across borders."

Mia opened the folder to find photographs and documents detailing a prominent Barcelona art dealer, Felix Duarte. His gallery had long been known for its eclectic and sophisticated collection of both contemporary and historical art. He was a familiar face at high-profile exhibitions, and his reputation had appeared untarnished.

"Duarte? I can't believe it," Mia said, her brow furrowed. "He's always presented himself as an advocate for transparency in the market."

Llorente leaned forward, his tone measured. "We've verified several payments connected to the smuggling operation through his gallery. It's clear he's been leveraging his reputation to facilitate these deals under the radar."

"What's our next step?" Mia asked, her resolve strengthening.

"We need to approach this carefully," Llorente replied. "Duarte is well-connected, and we can't afford to alert him prematurely. We'll start by surveying his gallery and gathering as much information as possible."

Mia agreed to assist, knowing her familiarity with the art community would be invaluable. Over the next several days, she and Llorente posed as potential buyers, carefully probing Duarte for signs of his involvement. They noticed subtle clues—a willingness to evade questions about provenance, vague explanations for certain acquisitions, and frequent consultations with suspicious intermediaries.

After gathering sufficient evidence, Llorente and Sophie set up a sting operation to catch Duarte in the act. Mia played a crucial role, posing as a collector interested in acquiring a rare piece known to be in Duarte's inventory. The piece in question had been smuggled from a private collection abroad, and Duarte was eager to broker a deal.

The day of the sting was tense. Mia entered the gallery, every detail meticulously planned to lure Duarte into revealing his role. As she negotiated with him over the price and provenance, the dealer became increasingly confident, boasting about his network of contacts and his ability to move valuable items discreetly.

At the peak of the conversation, Llorente and his team intervened, catching Duarte off guard. They confiscated the smuggled artwork and arrested Duarte on charges of trafficking in illegal art.

Back at her studio later that evening, Mia reflected on the operation. The arrest of Felix Duarte sent shockwaves through the art community, serving as a stark reminder of the ongoing fight against corruption. It marked another chapter in Mia's journey, one that reinforced her dedication to her mission.

Her next painting was a vibrant tribute to the triumph of truth over deceit, its colors swirling in a harmonious blend of passion and purpose. As she laid the final strokes on the canvas, Mia felt the weight of her journey, knowing that while the path ahead remained fraught with challenges, she would continue to fight for a world where art could thrive untainted.

# Chapter 34: Cracks in the Gallery

After the arrest of Felix Duarte, the art world seemed to hold its breath. The gallery owner's dramatic downfall sent ripples of anxiety through both reputable and questionable dealers, shaking the foundations of trust that held the industry together. Investigations in Barcelona and beyond grew more urgent, and Inspector Llorente's team became inundated with new leads, many of which pointed to a broader conspiracy.

Mia found herself at the epicenter of these efforts, balancing her dual roles as artist and investigator with growing skill and tenacity. Her involvement in the sting operation had solidified her reputation as a force for good, but it also made her a target for those still operating in the shadows.

One evening, as she was wrapping up a meeting with Sophie Renaud at her studio, Mia noticed a car idling on the street below, its headlights briefly illuminating her windows before disappearing into the night. The following day, she found her mailbox stuffed with vaguely threatening notes, all urging her to stop "meddling where she didn't belong."

When Mia shared her concerns with Llorente, he insisted on increasing security around her studio and home. "We can't take chances now, Mia. Your safety is paramount."

Despite the growing threats, Mia remained resolute. She continued her work with unwavering determination, knowing that the cracks she had helped expose in Duarte's gallery were just the beginning. The information gathered from his arrest pointed to a complex network of collaborators, each one complicit in laundering stolen art through seemingly legitimate channels.

Sophie and Llorente worked tirelessly to compile evidence, linking Duarte to several high-profile galleries across Europe and Asia. As the puzzle pieces fell into place, a pattern emerged, revealing a sophisticated web that used art as currency to fund illicit activities.

One of Duarte's former associates, eager to escape a harsher sentence, provided key information about an upcoming shipment. This shipment would serve as the final nail in the network's coffin if intercepted.

The operation to intercept the shipment was delicate and required Mia's expertise to identify the artworks swiftly. The team prepared meticulously, their nerves stretched thin as the clock ticked down to the fateful night.

At last, the evening came. In the dimly lit warehouse near the Barcelona docks, Mia, Llorente, and Sophie waited in silence as the shipment was unloaded. The tension was palpable as they watched the figures moving crates and containers.

When the time was right, the police swept in, seizing the entire shipment and arresting those involved. Mia was brought in to identify and catalogue the recovered pieces, her heart racing with adrenaline. Each piece she examined told a story of theft, deceit, and greed, but her steady hands and sharp eye brought order to the chaos.

By dawn, the operation had concluded, and the authorities had everything they needed to dismantle the forgery network. Felix Duarte's arrest had been the catalyst, and now the entire structure was poised to collapse. The team knew the end was near for this chapter of deception.

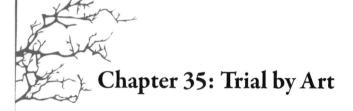

# Chapter 35: Trial by Art

The successful interception of the shipment was a turning point, shifting the momentum decidedly in favor of Mia, Inspector Llorente, and Sophie Renaud. The confiscated artifacts were the final pieces of evidence that solidified the case against the forgery network. As the authorities meticulously traced each item back to its origin, the net tightened around those who had thrived in the underbelly of the art world.

The ensuing weeks were a whirlwind of preparations as Mia worked closely with law enforcement and legal teams to ensure the upcoming trials were airtight. Her expertise and careful documentation of each artifact provided the clarity needed to confirm their stolen status, and her testimony was instrumental in linking the defendants to their illicit operations.

The trial, held in Barcelona, was a media spectacle. Reporters from around the world gathered to cover the proceedings, which would determine the fate of some of the most influential figures in the art world. Felix Duarte, facing multiple charges of smuggling and money laundering, was among those who stood before the judge, his once-confident demeanor shattered by the overwhelming evidence against him.

Mia sat quietly in the gallery, her presence a reminder of the unwavering determination that had brought these criminals to justice. The courtroom buzzed with tension as witness after witness testified, painting a grim picture of deceit and betrayal. When it was Mia's turn, she took the stand with a steady resolve.

Through detailed explanations, she revealed the network's inner workings and how seemingly reputable galleries had turned into conduits for stolen art. Her calm, authoritative demeanor left little room for doubt, and her visual aids of recovered artifacts helped the jury understand the magnitude of the operation.

After weeks of testimony, cross-examinations, and final arguments, the jury returned its verdict: guilty on all counts. The sentencing was harsh but justified, delivering a message that art was not a commodity to be exploited for greed. Felix Duarte and his associates were to serve long prison terms, and their galleries were confiscated and dismantled.

After the trial, as Mia left the courthouse, she felt a sense of closure but also a hint of sadness for the art community that had been betrayed. Inspector Llorente joined her outside, a weary smile on his face. "It's over, Mia. You did it."

"We did it," Mia corrected, returning his smile. "But it's not over, not really. There will always be those who try to exploit art, but now we've shown that there are people who will fight to protect it."

Sophie Renaud approached them, extending her hand to Mia. "You've set a new standard for what it means to protect our cultural heritage. Your work has inspired countless others to step up."

With the shadow of the trial finally lifting, Mia knew that her role as an artist and advocate was far from finished. The journey had been difficult and fraught with danger, but she had learned that art was worth fighting for—worth protecting for future generations.

Returning to her studio, Mia found solace in the familiar rhythms of her brushes on canvas. The story she had told was now behind her, but new stories waited to unfold, and she was ready to face them with the same unwavering resolve that had brought down a criminal empire.

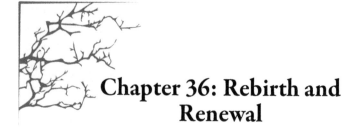

# Chapter 36: Rebirth and Renewal

After the trial, the art world was left to rebuild. The ripples of the forgery network's collapse extended far beyond Barcelona, and galleries and collectors everywhere began reevaluating their own practices. With Felix Duarte and his associates serving their sentences, confidence was slowly restored, and efforts to protect cultural heritage gained renewed momentum.

Mia found herself in high demand as galleries sought her advice on verifying their collections. She worked closely with cultural organizations to develop new standards for provenance research and offered workshops to help young artists understand the importance of integrity in their work.

One bright morning, as Mia stood in her studio contemplating her next artistic project, a knock on the door interrupted her reverie. Inspector Llorente entered, his expression relaxed and warm, a stark contrast to the intensity of their previous meetings.

"Mia," he greeted, "I've come to deliver some good news."

"Oh? What's that?" she asked, curiosity piqued.

"The authorities have managed to trace and recover even more artifacts linked to Duarte's network. They've been returned to their rightful owners, and several national museums have already offered to help restore some of the damaged pieces."

Mia's face lit up with satisfaction. "That's wonderful news, Carlos. I'm glad to hear that some good is coming from this."

Llorente nodded, a knowing smile playing on his lips. "Your efforts made it possible. You brought attention to the importance of preserving art for future generations."

As he departed, Mia turned her attention back to her studio. The events of the past year had shifted her perspective, and she felt compelled to capture that journey on canvas. Her new series, which she titled "Rebirth and Renewal," was a vivid expression of light overcoming darkness. Each piece conveyed a story of triumph and resilience, woven through intricate layers of color and symbolism.

In the weeks that followed, the series attracted significant attention, culminating in an invitation for a solo exhibition at one of Barcelona's most prestigious galleries. The opening night was a celebration of art's power to unite, heal, and inspire. The gallery was packed with collectors, artists, and law enforcement officers who had been part of Mia's journey.

As Mia moved through the crowd, she was approached by Sophie Renaud. "Your work speaks volumes, Mia," Sophie said warmly. "It's a reminder of why we fight for art and all it represents."

"Thank you, Sophie," Mia replied. "It's a message that needs to be heard."

The evening continued with animated conversations about the future of art preservation, and Mia realized that she had not only found her voice but had also given others the courage to speak up for what mattered. Her art had evolved beyond the confines of her studio, becoming a force that influenced minds and policies alike.

In the quiet that followed the exhibition's closing, Mia stood alone among her paintings, absorbing the impact of what had been achieved. Her studio, once a place of solitude, had become a hub of change. The canvases that surrounded her were no longer just expressions of her artistic vision but living embodiments of her journey to safeguard truth and integrity in art.

With a deep breath, she picked up her brush and prepared a new canvas. There were more stories to tell, more layers to uncover. The fight for art and culture would never truly end, but Mia knew she was ready to meet whatever challenges came her way with unwavering dedication and hope.

# Chapter 37: The Dawn of Truth

Mia's journey from an unsuspecting artist preparing for her first exhibit to a key figure in dismantling a global forgery network had fundamentally reshaped her view of the art world. She had stood up against corruption and emerged victorious, her name now synonymous with integrity and resilience.

With the echoes of the trial fading, life gradually returned to normal. The arts community began to heal, though scars of betrayal and lost trust remained. Many galleries and collectors were more vigilant than ever, implementing stringent checks to prevent similar criminal activities. Inspector Llorente and Sophie Renaud continued their vigilance in the fight against art crime, often seeking Mia's advice on developing strategies for future cases.

Meanwhile, Mia took time to reflect on the journey she'd been through. One morning, as the sun poured through her studio windows, she stood before a blank canvas and felt a wave of optimism wash over her. It was a new beginning, a moment of rebirth where the memories of the past could be transformed into something hopeful.

She spent days meticulously working on a new series called "The Dawn of Truth." The paintings carried an air of optimism, each piece representing the triumph of authenticity over deception. Lush greens and vibrant blues swirled together with touches of gold and crimson, creating compositions that conveyed her unwavering belief in art's potential to heal and inspire.

During this period, Mia also worked with cultural institutions to establish a foundation dedicated to supporting emerging artists and promoting art education. The foundation's initiatives aimed to nurture creativity while emphasizing the importance of integrity in artistic expression. She believed that by instilling these values in the next generation, the foundations of a better art world could be laid.

Months later, Mia's new series was exhibited at her own gallery in Barcelona, drawing a diverse crowd of supporters, critics, and friends. Among them were Inspector Llorente and Sophie Renaud, who had been unwavering allies through the trials and triumphs.

"You've done it again, Mia," Llorente said, admiring one of her vibrant canvases. "This work embodies everything you've fought for."

"Thank you, Carlos. It's been quite the journey," Mia replied with a smile, glancing around the room at the lively conversations and shared enthusiasm.

Sophie joined them, a glass of wine in hand. "Your foundation will make a lasting impact, Mia. It's a testament to what can be achieved with passion and dedication."

The night was a celebration of resilience and a new beginning, marking the end of one chapter and the start of another. Mia's name would forever be associated with truth and determination, a legacy she had built through perseverance and integrity.

As the evening drew to a close, Mia returned to her studio, surrounded by her work. The journey had changed her, but it had also reaffirmed her unwavering belief in the power of art. She knew there were more challenges ahead, more stories to tell, but for now, she was content in the knowledge that she had made a difference, one brushstroke at a time.

# Chapter 38: A New Vision

In the wake of her latest exhibition, "The Dawn of Truth," Mia felt a sense of accomplishment and fulfillment. The art world was beginning to stabilize, and her foundation had already started to gain traction, providing support and mentorship to emerging artists who were eager to leave their mark on the world. Her tireless advocacy for transparency and her fight against art crime had set a new standard in the industry, but Mia knew there was more work to be done.

One bright morning, as she walked through the foundation's office reviewing proposals and meeting with her team, she felt a renewed sense of purpose. The sunlit space buzzed with energy as curators and administrators worked tirelessly to identify promising artists and organize educational workshops.

Sophie Renaud arrived with exciting news. "We've been approached by several museums across Europe interested in collaborating on a traveling exhibition about the preservation of cultural heritage. They want you to curate it."

Mia's eyes lit up at the prospect. "What an incredible opportunity! We'd be able to reach so many people and share the importance of art protection globally."

"The idea is to feature authentic artifacts alongside pieces that were recovered from the forgery networks," Sophie continued. "This way, people can see how easily one can be deceived and understand the importance of proper authentication."

As they brainstormed ideas, Mia envisioned an exhibition that would not only celebrate the beauty of cultural artifacts but also educate and inspire a new generation to value authenticity. It would be a collaboration between curators, historians, and law enforcement experts, each offering unique insights into the challenges of preserving the world's artistic legacy.

Months later, the first leg of the exhibition opened at a prestigious museum in Paris. Entitled "Guardians of Culture," the exhibit was a resounding success, attracting art enthusiasts, students, and professionals alike. Each display told a story of resilience and vigilance, illustrating how truth prevailed despite the forces of greed and deceit. Mia curated the collection carefully, blending history and education with a captivating narrative.

Inspector Llorente, Sophie Renaud, and several other key collaborators were present at the grand opening, marveling at the way Mia had brought everything together. "You've created something truly special here, Mia," Llorente said, taking in the exhibit's intricate layout.

Sophie nodded in agreement. "This exhibition is already having an impact, and it's just the beginning. The message is clear: the art world will stand strong against corruption."

As the exhibit traveled to other major cities, the response was overwhelmingly positive. "Guardians of Culture" became a rallying cry for those who valued transparency and accountability in art. It brought renewed attention to the importance of protecting cultural heritage and encouraged new policies and collaborations across the industry.

Back in Barcelona, Mia continued her work with the foundation, mentoring young artists and promoting her vision of an art world where authenticity reigned supreme. Her journey had taken her from a quiet painter focused on her first exhibition to a globally recognized curator and advocate.

In the peaceful solitude of her studio, Mia reflected on the path she'd walked and the countless individuals who had stood by her along the way. The world of art had changed irrevocably since she first took up her brush, but she knew that its true beauty lay in its capacity for renewal and rebirth.

Mia dipped her brush into a pool of vibrant paint, her heart filled with hope and inspiration. There were new stories to tell, new challenges to overcome, and she would continue to face them with the same courage and passion that had guided her all along.

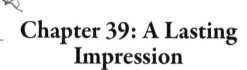

# Chapter 39: A Lasting Impression

The success of "Guardians of Culture" reverberated across the global art community, solidifying Mia's legacy as an advocate for integrity and education. The exhibition traveled to more cities, each stop sparking conversations about the value of art preservation and the power of truth. Students, artists, and collectors all engaged with the narrative Mia had woven, learning not just to admire art but to protect its legacy.

Back at the foundation's headquarters in Barcelona, the energy was palpable. Mia's team worked tirelessly to support their growing network of emerging artists and organize new programs that promoted transparency in the industry. They had become a beacon for those seeking guidance and mentorship, and Mia found great joy in sharing her experiences and insights with those beginning their own journeys.

One day, Inspector Llorente and Sophie Renaud paid a visit to Mia's studio, bearing a small gift: a finely crafted box of pastels. "A small token of appreciation," Llorente said with a smile. "For the artist who has painted a brighter future for us all."

Mia accepted the gift gratefully, the sentiment behind it touching her deeply. "Thank you both for your unwavering support. I couldn't have done this without you."

Sophie looked around at the canvases leaning against the walls, each one a testament to Mia's vision and dedication. "So, what's next for you, Mia?"

Mia paused, her gaze drifting to a blank canvas that stood in the corner. "There's still so much to be done, but I've been thinking about a new series that explores the interconnectedness of art, history, and society. I want to capture how these elements shape each other across time."

Llorente nodded thoughtfully. "It sounds like a remarkable project, Mia. I have no doubt you'll bring the same passion and clarity to it that you've shown in everything else."

Over the following weeks, Mia poured herself into her new series. She drew inspiration from her journey and the countless individuals she had met along the way. Each painting captured a different facet of the relationship between art and history: the vibrant exchange of ideas, the subtle influence of culture on creativity, and the enduring nature of artistic expression.

As the canvases filled her studio, the series took shape, revealing a story of resilience and interconnectedness. Mia knew this work would serve as a reminder that art was not just a reflection of the world, but a living force that could shape it for the better.

In the months that followed, Mia exhibited her new series at her gallery, drawing visitors who marveled at the intricate interplay of color, texture, and symbolism. Her work was hailed as a masterpiece, a testament to her ability to convey complex themes with grace and nuance.

One evening, as she stood alone in the gallery, surrounded by her paintings, Mia reflected on the journey that had brought her here. She had faced challenges and dangers she could never have imagined but had emerged stronger and more determined than ever to make a difference.

With a contented sigh, she left the gallery and returned to her studio, where the familiar scents of paint and turpentine welcomed her home. As she prepared a new canvas, she knew that her legacy would not only be defined by her triumphs over corruption but also by the hope and inspiration she had brought to those around her.

Art would continue to be her voice, her brush the instrument through which she told her stories. And as she began to paint once more, she knew that her lasting impression would be one of courage, authenticity, and the unwavering belief that beauty could indeed change the world.

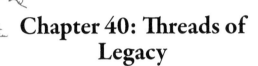

# Chapter 40: Threads of Legacy

The resonance of Mia's latest series lingered long after the final exhibit concluded. Her work had firmly established her not just as an artist but as a storyteller whose dedication to truth had fundamentally transformed the art world. She continued to mentor young artists through the foundation, ensuring that her philosophy of transparency and integrity permeated their education.

As her role expanded, she received a letter from the board of a renowned international museum. They wished to include her paintings as part of a new permanent collection, titled "Threads of Legacy," showcasing artists who had significantly influenced the preservation and evolution of art. It was an honor Mia never imagined she would receive, and she accepted it humbly.

The museum's collection featured her pivotal series, "The Dawn of Truth" and "Guardians of Culture," along with several key paintings from her latest work exploring the interconnectedness of art and society. Visitors from around the world walked through the halls, studying her canvases and reading about the remarkable story behind her journey.

Mia found herself giving more public lectures and collaborating with other artists and curators to strengthen networks of mentorship and preservation. Her once modest studio was now a vibrant center of activity, where ideas flowed freely and young talents found inspiration in her unwavering commitment to artistic values.

One evening, while organizing a series of educational workshops for emerging artists, Mia received a surprise visit from Inspector Llorente and Sophie Renaud. They greeted her warmly, bearing a beautifully framed photograph of the three of them standing together at the final exhibition of "Guardians of Culture."

"Mia, you've been the heart of everything we've accomplished," Llorente said. "This is just a small reminder of how grateful we are for your partnership and vision."

Mia smiled, deeply moved. "Thank you, Carlos. And thank you, Sophie. I wouldn't have achieved this without you."

Sophie glanced around the studio, appreciating the lively creative energy that filled the space. "The work you've started here will continue to inspire generations of artists and advocates for years to come."

As the trio reminisced, Mia reflected on how their collaboration had shifted the art world toward a brighter future. She knew the fight against art crime was ongoing, but they had laid a strong foundation to build upon.

Later that evening, after the studio had emptied and the quiet settled in, Mia stood before a blank canvas, her mind teeming with new ideas. The future was wide open, and there were still untold stories to explore. Her brushes, organized and ready, were like instruments awaiting the maestro's direction.

With a steady hand, she dipped her brush into a vivid blue and made the first stroke on the canvas, her heart light with the joy of creation and the knowledge that she was painting not just for herself but for a world that believed in the transformative power of art.

Every thread of legacy she painted was another step in her journey, a celebration of courage, creativity, and the beauty of truth that would continue to shape the world for generations to come.

# Don't miss out!

Visit the website below and you can sign up to receive emails whenever Adela Vesper publishes a new book. There's no charge and no obligation.

https://books2read.com/r/B-A-VQLJB-SQLED

**BOOKS 2 READ**

Connecting independent readers to independent writers.

# Also by Adela Vesper

Palette of Intrigue - A Female-Led Mystery Unveiling Barcelona Art Scene

Milton Keynes UK
Ingram Content Group UK Ltd.
UKHW020636140524
442690UK00001B/56